THE RUPA BOOK OF EERIE STORIES

Other Ruskin Bond Titles

Angry River
A Little Night Music
A Long Walk for Bina
Hanuman to the Rescue
Ghost Stories from the Raj
Strange Men, Strange Places
The India I Love
Tales and Legends from India
The Blue Umbrella
Ruskin Bond's Children's Omnibus
The Ruskin Bond Omnibus-I
The Ruskin Bond Omnibus-II
The Ruskin Bond Omnibus-III
The Ruskin Bond Omnibus-IV
The Ruskin Bond Omnibus-V
Rupa Book of Great Animal Stories
The Rupa Book of True Tales of Mystery and Adventure
The Rupa Book of Ruskin Bond's Himalayan Tales
The Rupa Book of Great Suspense Stories
The Rupa Laughter Omnibus
The Rupa Book of Scary Stories
The Rupa Book of Haunted Houses
The Rupa Book of Travellers' Tales
The Rupa Book of Great Crime Stories
The Rupa Book of Nightmare Tales
The Rupa Book of Shikar Stories
The Rupa Book of Love Stories
The Rupa Book of Wicked Stories
The Rupa Book of Heartwarming Stories
The Rupa Book of Thrills and Spills
Rendezvous With Horror
The Rupa Book of Spooky Encounters
Shudders in the Dark

THE RUPA BOOK OF EERIE STORIES

Edited by
Ruskin Bond

Rupa . Co

Published 2007 by

Rupa . Co

7/16, Ansari Road, Daryaganj,
New Delhi 110 002

Sales Centres:

Allahabad Bangalore Chandigarh
Chennai Hyderabad Jaipur Kathmandu
Kolkata Mumbai Pune

Typeset by
Mindways Design
1410 Chiranjiv Tower,
43 Nehru Place
New Delhi 110 019

Printed in India by
Saurabh Printers Pvt. Ltd.
A-16, Sector-IV,
Noida 201 301

Contents

Introduction

The one thing I've thoroughly enjoyed doing all my life is spinning tales that would captivate readers and make them ask for more. Hence, time to rummage through my archives and fish out this new set of stories—a rare compilation of chilling tales.

The stories in this collection are replete with terror, adventure, perils and thrills. Myriad themes run through them – the unknown, the uncanny, the nightmarish and the mysterious. Written by master story-tellers, known the world over, these intriguing tales seem to have an international flavour and cater to our affinities for the ghostly, supernatural elements around us.

Every old house has its own story. Bram Stoker's 'The Judge's House' seems to convey the strong emanations from the past that will send a shudder down your spine. Hugh Walpole's school story, 'Jeremy and the Runaways', is another original work, a sure-shot page-turner portraying a boy's courage and dilemma.

There is no ghost in Phyllis Bottome's 'Henry', but it is frightening all the same. Other gifted writers in this collection are E.F. Benson, who discovers a vampire in a sleepy English village, and Gerald Kersh, who takes you to a fascinating 'Carnival on the Downs'. C.A.Kincaid, on the other hand, tells us a terrifying story of an Indian werewolf.

Beautifully crafted, this collection of unforgettable tales of human and superhuman encounter is a treat for readers. Each one conveys a sense of the spooky or the paranormal. And to enjoy these to the fullest, take this veteran's advice – read these gripping narratives preferably at night. The rich cast of characters will surely cast their magical spell on you. Reading each one of them will be an enriching experience.

Happy reading!!

Ruskin Bond

The Judge's House

BRAM STOKER

When the time for his examination drew near, Malcolm Malcolmson made up his mind to go somewhere to read by himself. He feared the attractions of the seaside, and also he feared complete rural isolation, for of old he knew its charms, and so he determined to find some unpretentious little town where there would be nothing to distract him. He refrained from asking suggestions from any of his friends, for he argued that each would recommend some place of which he had knowledge, and where he had already acquaintances. As Malcolmson wished to avoid friends, he had no wish to encumber himself with the attention of friends' friends, and so he determined to look out for a place for himself. He packed a portmanteau with some clothes and all the books he required, and then took ticket for the first name on the local time-table which he did not know.

When at the end of three hours' journey he alighted at Benchurch, he felt satisfied that he had so far obliterated his tracks as to be sure of having a peaceful opportunity of pursuing his studies. He went straight to the one in which the sleepy little place contained and put up for the night. Benchurch was a market-town, and once in three weeks was crowded to excess, but for the remainder of the twenty–one days it was as attractive as a desert. Malcolmson looked around the day after his arrival to try to find quarters more isolated than even so quiet an inn as 'The Good Traveller' afforded. There was only one place which took his fancy, and it certainly satisfied his wildest ideas regarding quiet; in fact, quiet was not the proper word to apply to it—desolation was the only term conveying any suitable idea of its isolation. It was an old rambling, heavy-built house of the Jacobean style, with heavy gables and windows, unusually small, and set higher than was customary in such houses, and was surrounded with a high brick wall massively built. Indeed, on examination it looked more like a fortified house than an ordinary dwelling. But all these things pleased Malcolmson. 'Here,' he thought, 'is the very spot I have been looking for, and if I can only get opportunity of using it I shall be happy.' His joy was increased when he realised beyond doubt that it was not at present inhabited.

From the post-office he got the name of the agent, who was rarely surprised at the application to rent a part of the old house. Mr Carnford, the local lawyer and agent, was a genial old gentleman, and frankly confessed his delight at anyone being willing to live in the house.

'To tell you the truth,' said he, 'I should be only too happy, on behalf of the owners, to let anyone have the house rent free for a term of years if only to accustom the people here to see it inhabited. It has been so long empty that some kind of absurd prejudice has grown up about it, and this can be best put down by its occupation—if only,' he added with a sly glance at Malcomson, 'by a scholar like yourself, who wants its quiet for a time.'

Malcolmson thought it needless to ask the agent about the 'absurd prejudice'; he knew he would get more information, if he should require it, on that subject from other quarters. He paid his three months' rent, got a receipt, and the name of an old woman who would probably undertake to 'do' for him, and came away with the keys in his pocket. He then went to the landlady of the inn, who was a cheerful and most kindly person, and asked her advice as to such stores and provisions as he would be likely to require. She threw up her hands in amazement when he told her where he was going to settle himself.

'Not in the Judge's House!' she said, and grew pale as she spoke. He explained the locality of the house, saying that he did not know its name. When he had finished she answered:

'Aye, sure enough—sure enough the very place! It is the Judge's House sure enough.' He asked her to tell him about the place, why so called, and what there was against it. She told him that it was so called locally because it had been many years before—how long she could not say, as she was herself from another part of the country, but she thought it must have been a hundred years or more—the abode of a judge who was held in great terror on account of his harsh sentences and hostility to prisoners at Assizes. As to what there was against the house itself, she could not tell. She had often asked, but no one could inform her; but there was a general feeling that there was *something*, and for her own part she would not take all the money in Drinkwarter's Bank and stay in the house an hour by herself. Then she apologised to Malcolmson for her disturbing talk.

'It is too bad of me, sir, and you—and a young gentleman, too—if you will pardon me saying it, going to live there all alone. If you were my boy—and you'll excuse me for saying it—you wouldn't sleep there a night, not if I had to go there myself and pull the big alarm bell that's on the roof!' The good creature was so manifestly in earnest, and was so kindly in her intentions, that Malcolmson, although amused, was touched. He told her kindly how much he appreciated her interest in him, and added:

'But, my dear Mrs Witham, indeed you need not be concerned about me! A man who is reading for the Mathematical Tripos has too much to think of to be disturbed by any of these mysterious "somethings", and his work is of too exact and prosaic a kind to allow of his having any corner in his mind for mysteries of any kind. Harmonical Progression, Permutations and Combinations, and Elliptic Functions have sufficient mysteries for me!' Mrs Witham kindly undertook to see after his commissions, and he went himself to look for the old woman who had been recommended to him. When he returned to the Judge's House with her, after an interval of a couple of hours, he found Mrs Witham herself waning with several men and boys carrying parcels, and an upholsterer's man with a bed in a cart, for she said, though tables and chairs might be all very well, a bed that hadn't been aired for mayhap fifty years was not proper for young bones to lie on. She was evidently curious to see the inside of the house; and though manifestly so afraid of the 'somethings' that at the slightest sound she clutched on to Malcolmson, whom she never left for a moment, she went over the whole place.

After his examination of the house, Malcolmson decided to take up his abode in the great dining-room, which was big enough to serve for all his requirements; and Mrs Witham, with the aid of the charwoman, Mrs Dempster, proceeded to arrange matters. When the hampers were brought in and unpacked, Malcolmson saw that with much kind forethought she had sent from her own kitchen sufficient provisions to last for a few days. Before going she expressed all sorts of kind wishes, and at the door turned and said:

'And perhaps, sir, as the room is big and draughty it might be well to have one of those big screens put round your bed at night—though, truth to tell, I would die myself if I were to be so shut in with all kinds of—of "things", that put their heads round the sides, or over the top, and look on me!' The image which she had called up was too much for her nerves, and she fled incontinently.

Mrs Dempster sniffed in a superior manner as the landlady disappeared and remarked that for her own part she wasn't afraid of all the bogies in the kingdom.

'I'll tell you what it is, sir,' she said, 'bogies is all kinds and sorts of things—except bogies! Rats and mice, and beetles; and creaky doors, and loose slates, and broken panes, and stiff drawer handles, that stay out when you pull them and then fall down in the middle of the night. Look at the wainscot of the room! It is old—hundreds of years old! Do you think there's no rats and beetles there! And do you imagine, sir, that you won't see none of them! Rats is bogies, I tell you and bogies is rats; and don't you get to think anything else!'

'Mrs Dempster,' said Malcolmson gravely, making her a polite bow, 'you know more than a Senior Wrangler! And let me say that as a mark of esteem for your indubitable soundness of head and heart, I shall, when I go, give you possession of this house, and let you stay here by yourself for the last two months of my tenancy, for four weeks will serve my purpose.'

'Thank you kindly, sir!' she answered, 'but I couldn't sleep away from home a night. I am in Greenhow's Charity, and if I slept a night away from my rooms I should lose all I have got to live on. The rules is very strict; and there's too many watching for a vacancy for me to run any risks in the matter. Only for that, sir, I'd gladly come here and attend on you altogether during your stay.'

'My good woman,' said Malcolmson hastily, 'I have come here on purpose to obtain solitude; and believe me that I am grateful to the late Greenhow for having so organised his admirable charity—whatever it is—that I am perforce denied the opportunity of suffering from such a form of temptation! Saint Anthony himself could not be more rigid on the point!'

The old woman laughed harshly. 'Ah, you young gentlemen,' she said, 'you don't fear for naught; and belike you'll get all the solitude you want here.' She set to work with her cleaning; and by nightfall, when Malcolmson returned from his walk—he always had one of his books to study as he walked—he found the room swept and tidied, a fire burning in the old hearth, the lamp lit, and the table spread for supper with Mrs Witham's excellent fare. 'This is comfort, indeed,' he said, as he rubbed his hands.

When he had finished his supper and lifted the tray to the other end of the great oak dining-table, he got out his books again, put fresh wood on the fire, trimmed his lamp, and set himself down to a spell of real hard work. He went on without pause till about eleven o'clock, when he knocked off for a bit to fix his fire and lamp and to make himself a cup of tea. He had always been a tea-drinker, and during his college life had sat late at work and had taken tea late. The rest was a great luxury to him, and he enjoyed it with a sense of delicious, voluptuous ease. The renewed fire leaped and sparkled and threw quaint shadows through the great old room; and as he sipped his hot tea, he revelled in the sense of isolation from his kind. Then it was that he began to notice for the first time what a noise the rats were making.

'Surely,' he thought, 'they cannot have been at it all the time I was reading. Had they been, I must have noticed it!' Presently, when the noise increased, he satisfied himself that it was really new. It was evident that at first the rats had been frightened at the presence of a stranger and the light of fire and lamp, but that as the time went on, they had grown bolder and were now disporting themselves as was their wont.

How busy they were! And hark to the strange noises! Up and down behind the old wainscot, over the ceiling and under the floor they raced, and gnawed, and scratched! Malcolmson smiled to himself as he recalled to mind the saying of Mrs Dempster, 'Bogies is rats, and rats is bogies!' The tea began to have its effect of intellectual and nervous stimulus; he saw with joy another long spell of work to be done before the night was past, and in the sense of security which it gave him, he allowed himself the luxury of a good look round the room. He took his lamp in one hand and went all around, wondering that so quaint and beautiful an old house had been so long neglected. The carving of the oak on the panels of the wainscot was fine, and on and round the doors and windows it was beautiful and of rare merit. There were some old pictures on the walls, but they were coated so thick with dust and dirt that he could not distinguish any detail of them, though he held his lamp as high as he could over his head. Here and there, as he went round, he saw some crack or hole blocked for a moment by the face of a rat with its bright eyes glittering in the light, but in an instant it was gone, and a squeak and a scamper followed.

The thing that most struck him, however, was the rope of the great alarm bell on the roof, which hung down in a corner of the room on the right-hand side of the fireplace. He pulled up close to the hearth a great high-backed carved oak chair, and sat down to his last cup of tea. When this was done, he made up the fire and went back to his work, sitting at the corner of the table, having the fire to his left. For a while the rats disturbed him somewhat with their perpetual scampering, but he got accustomed to the noise as one does to the ticking of a clock or to the roar of moving water; and he became so immersed in his work that everything in the world, except the problem which he was trying to solve, passed away from him.

He suddenly looked up; his problem was still unsolved, and there was in the air that sense of the hour before the dawn, which is a dread to doubtful life. The noise of the rats had ceased. Indeed it seemed to him that it must have ceased but lately, and that it was the sudden cessation which had disturbed him. The fire had fallen low, but still it threw out a deep red glow. As he looked he started in spite of his *sang froid*.

There on the great high-backed carved oak chair by the right side of the fireplace sat an enormous rat, steadily glaring at him with baleful eyes. He made a motion to it as though to hunt it away, but it did not stir. Then he made the motion of throwing something. Still it did not stir, but showed its great white teeth angrily, and its cruel eyes shone in the lamplight with an added vindictiveness.

Malcolmson felt amazed, and seizing the poker from the hearth ran at it to kill it. Before, however, he could strike it, the rat, with a squeak that sounded like the concentration of hate, jumped upon the floor, and running up the rope of the alarm bell disappeared in the darkness beyond the range of the green-shaded lamp. Instantly, strange to say, the noisy scampering of the rats in the wainscot began again.

By this time Malcolmson's mind was quite off the problem; and as a shrill cock-crow outside told him of the approach of morning, he went to bed to sleep.

He slept so sound that he was not even waked by Mrs Dempster coming in to make up his room. It was only when she had tidied up the place and got his breakfast ready, and tapped on the screen which closed in his bed, that he woke. He was a little tired still after his night's hard work, but a strong cup of tea soon freshened him up, and, taking his book, he went out for his morning walk, bringing with him a few sandwiches lest he should not care to return till dinner time. He found a quiet walk between high elms some way outside the town, and here he spent the greater part of the day studying his Laplace. On his return he looked in to see Mrs Witham and to thank her for her kindness. When she saw him coming through the diamond-paned bay-window of her sanctum, she came out to meet him and asked him in. She looked at him searchingly and shook her head as she said:

'You must not overdo it, sir. You are paler this morning than you should be. Too late hours and too hard work on the brain isn't good for any man! But tell me, sir, how did you pass the night? Well, I hope? But, my heart! sir, I was glad when Mrs Dempster told me this morning that you were all right and sleeping sound when she went in.'

'Oh, I was all right,' he answered, smiling, 'the "somethings" didn't worry me, as yet. Only the rats; and they had a circus, I tell you, all over the place. There was one wicked-looking old devil that sat up on my own chair by the fire, and wouldn't go till I took the poker to him, and then he ran up the rope of the alarm bell and got to somewhere up the wall or the ceiling—I couldn't see where, it was so dark.'

'Mercy on us,' said Mrs Witham, 'an old devil, and sitting on a chair by the fireside! Take care, sir! Take care! There's many a true word spoken in jest.'

'How do you mean? 'pon my word I don't understand.'

'An old devil! The old devil, perhaps. There! sir, you needn't laugh,' for Malcolmson had broken into a hearty peal. 'You young folks thinks it easy to laugh at things that makes older ones shudder. Never mind, sir,! Never mind! Please God, you'll laugh all the time. It's what I wish you myself!' and the good lady beamed all over in sympathy with his enjoyment, her fears gone for a moment.

'Oh, forgive me!' said Malcolmson presently. 'Don't think me rude; but the idea was too much for me—that the old devil himself was on the chair last night!' And at the thought he laughed again. Then he went home to dinner.

This evening the scampering of the rats began earlier; indeed it had been going on before his arrival, and only ceased whilst his presence by its freshness disturbed them. After dinner he sat by the fire for a while and had a smoke; and then, having cleared his table, began to work as before. To-night the rats disturbed him more than they had done on the previous night. How they scampered up and down and under and over! How they squeaked, and scratched, and gnawed! How they, getting bolder by degrees, came to the mouths of their holes and to the chinks and cracks and crannies in the wainscoting till their eyes shone like tiny lamps as the firelight rose and fell. But to him, now doubtless accustomed to them, their eyes were not wicked; only their playfulness touched him. Sometimes the boldest of them made sallies out on the floor or along the mouldings of the wainscot. Now and again as they disturbed him, Malcolmson made a sound to frighten them, smiting the table with his hand or giving a fierce 'Hsh, hsh,' so that they fled straightway to their holes.

And so the early part of the night wore on; and despite the noise, Malcolmson got more and more immersed in his work.

All at once he stopped, as on the previous night, being overcome by a sudden sense of silence. There was not the faintest sound of gnaw, or scratch, or squeak. The silence was as of the grave. He remembered the odd occurrence of the previous night, and instinctively he looked at the chair standing close by the fireside. And then a very odd sensation thrilled through him.

There, on the great old high-backed carved oak chair beside the fireplace sat the same enormous rat, steadily glaring at him with baleful eyes.

Instinctively he took the nearest thing to his hand, a book of logarithms, and flung it at it. The book was badly aimed and the rat did not stir, so again the poker performance of the previous night was repeated; and again the rat, being closely pursued, fled up the rope of the alarm bell. Strangely too, the departure of this rat was instantly followed by the renewal of the noise made by the general rat community. On this occasion, as on the previous one, Malcolmson could not see at what part of the room the rat disappeared, for the green shade of his lamp left the upper part of the room in darkness, and the fire had burned low.

On looking at his watch he found it was close to midnight; and, not sorry for the *divertissement*, he made up his fire and made himself his nightly pot of tea. He had got through a good spell of work, and thought himself entitled to a cigarette; and so he sat on the great carved oak chair before the fire and enjoyed it. Whilst smoking he began to think that he would like to know where the rat disappeared to, for he had certain ideas of the morrow not entirely disconnected with a rat-trap. Accordingly, he lit another lamp and placed it so that it would shine well into the right-hand corner of the wall by the fireplace. Then he got all the books he had with him, and placed them handy to throw at the vermin. Finally he lifted the rope of the alarm bell and placed the end of it on the table, fixing the extreme end under the lamp. As he handled it he could not help noticing how pliable it was, especially for so strong a rope, and one not in use. 'You could hang a man with it,' he thought to himself. When his preparations were made he looked around, and said complacently:

'There now, my friend, I think we shall learn something of you this time!' He began his work again, and though as before somewhat disturbed at first by the noise of the rats, soon lost himself in his propositions and problems.

Again, he was called to his immediate surroundings suddenly. This time it might not have been the sudden silence only which took his attention; there was a slight movement of the rope, and the lamp moved. Without stirring, he looked to see if his pile of books was within range, and then cast his eye along the rope.

As he looked he saw the great rat drop from the rope on the oak armchair and sit there glaring at him. He raised a book in his right hand, and taking careful aim, flung it at the rat. The latter, with a quick movement, sprang aside and dodged the missile. He then took another book, and a third, and flung them one after another at the rat, but each time unsuccessfully. At last, as he stood with a book poised in his hand to throw, the rat squeaked and seemed afraid. This made Malcolmson more than ever eager to strike, and the book flew and struck the rat a resounding blow. It gave a terrified squeak, and turning on its pursuer a look of terrible malevolence, ran up the chair-back and made a great jump to the rope of the alarm bell and ran up it like lightning. The lamp rocked under the sudden strain, but it was a heavy one and did not topple over. Malcolmson kept his eyes on the rat and saw it by the light of the second lamp leap to a moulding of the wainscot and disappear through a hole in one of the great pictures which hung on the wall, obscured and invisible through its coating of dirt and dust.

'I shall look up my friends' habitation in the morning,' said the student, as he went over to collect his books. 'The third picture from the fireplace; I shall not forget.' He picked up the books one by one, commenting on them as he lifted them. '*Conic Sections* he does not mind, nor *Cycloidal Oscillations,* nor the *Principia,* nor *Quaternions*, nor *Thermodynamics.* Now for the book that fetched him!' Malcolmson took it up and looked at it. As he did so he started, and a sudden pallor overspread his face. He looked round uneasily and shivered slightly, as he murmured to himself:

'The Bible my mother gave me! What an odd coincidence.' He sat down to work again, and the rats in the wainscot renewed their gambols. They did not disturb him, however; somehow their presence gave him a sense of companionship. But he could not attend to his work, and after striving to master the subject on which he was engaged, he gave it up in despair, and went to bed as the first streak of dawn stole in through the eastern window.

He slept heavily but uneasily, and dreamed much; and when Mrs Dempster woke him late in the morning, he seemed ill at ease, and for a few minutes did not seem to realise exactly where he was. His first request rather surprised the servant.

'Mrs Dempster, when I am out to-day I wish you would get the steps and dust or wash those pictures—especially that one the third from the fireplace—I want to see what they are.'

Late in the afternoon Malcolmson worked at his books in the shaded walk, and the cheerfulness of the previous day came back to him as the day wore on, and he found that his reading was progressing well. He had worked out to a satisfactory conclusion all the problems which had as yet baffled him, and it was in a state of jubilation that he paid a visit to Mrs Witham at 'The Good Traveller'. He found a stranger in the cosy sitting-room with the landlady, who was introduced to him as Dr Thornhill. She was not quite at ease, and this, combined with the Doctor's plunging at once into a series of questions, made Malcolmson come to the conclusion that his presence was not an accident, so without preliminary he said:

'Dr Thornhill, I shall with pleasure answer you any question you may choose to ask me if you will answer me one question first.'

The Doctor seemed surprised, but he smiled and answered at once. 'Done! What is it?'

'Did Mrs Witham ask you to come here and see me and advise me?'

Dr Thornhill for a moment was taken aback, and Mrs Witham got fiery red and turned away; but the doctor was a frank and ready man, and he answered at once and openly:

'She did: but she didn't intend you to know it. I suppose it was my clumsy haste that made you suspect. She told me that she did not like the idea of your being in that house all by yourself, and that she thought you took too much strong tea. In fact, she wants me to advise you if possible to give up the tea and the very late hours. I was a keen student in my time, so I suppose I may take the liberty of a college man, and without offence, advise you not quite as a stranger.'

Malcolmson with a bright smile held out his hand. 'Shake! as they say in America,' he said. 'I must thank you for your kindness and Mrs Witham too, and your kindness deserves a return on my part. I promise to take no more strong tea—no tea at all till you let me—and I shall go to bed to-night at one o'clock at the latest. Will that do?'

'Capital,' said the Doctor. 'Now tell us all that you noticed in the old house.' And so Malcolmson then and there told in minute detail all that had happened in the last two nights. He was interrupted every now and then by some exclamation from Mrs Witham, till finally when he told of the episode of the Bible, the landlady's pent-up emotions found vent in a shriek; and it was not till a stiff glass of brandy and water had been administered that she grew composed again. Dr Thornhill listened with a face of growing gravity, and when the narrative was complete and Mrs Witham had been restored, he asked:

'The rat always went up the rope of the alarm bell?'

'Always.'

'I suppose you know,' said the Doctor after a pause, 'what the rope is?'

'No!'

'It is,' said the Doctor slowly, 'the very rope which the hangman used for all the victims of the Judge's judicial rancour!' Here he was interrupted by another scream from Mrs Witham, and steps had to be taken for her recovery. Malcolmson, having looked at his watch and found that it was close to his dinner hour, had gone home before her complete recovery.

When Mrs Witham was herself again she almost assailed the Doctor with angry questions as to what he meant by putting such horrible ideas into the poor young man's mind. 'He has quite enough there already to upset him,' she added. Dr Thornhill replied:

'My dear madam, I had a distinct purpose in it! I wanted to draw his attention to the bell rope, and to fix it there. It may be that he is in a highly overwrought state, and has been studying too much, although I am bound to say that he seems as sound and healthy a young man, mentally and bodily, as ever I saw—but then the rats—and that suggestion of the devil.' The doctor shook his head and went on. 'I would have offered to go and stay the first night with him but that I felt sure it would have been a cause of offence. He may get in the night some strange fright or hallucination; and if he does, I want him to pull that rope. All alone as he is, it will give us warning, and we may reach him in time to be of service. I shall be sitting up pretty late to-night and shall keep my ears open. Do not be alarmed if Benchurch gets a surprise before morning.'

'Oh, Doctor, what do you mean? What do you mean?'

'I mean this; that possibly—nay, more probably—we shall hear the great alarm bell from the Judge's House to-night,' and the Doctor made about as effective an exit as could be thought of.

When Malcolmson arrived home he found that it was a little after his usual time, and Mrs Dempster had gone away—the rule of Greenhow's Charity were not to be neglected. He was glad to see that the place was bright and tidy with a cheerful fire and a well-trimmed lamp. The evening was colder than might have been expected in April, and a heavy wind was blowing with such rapidly-increasing strength that there was every promise of a storm during the night. For a few minutes after his entrance, the noise of the rats ceased; but so soon as they became accustomed to his presence they began again. He was glad to hear them, for he felt once more the feeling of companionship in their noise, and his mind ran back to the strange fact that they only ceased to manifest themselves when that other—the great rat with the baleful eyes—came upon the scene. The reading-lamp only was lit, and its green shade kept the ceiling and the upper part of the room in darkness, so that the cheerful light from the hearth spreading over the floor and shining on the white cloth laid over the end of the table was warm and cheery. Malcolmson sat down to his dinner with a good appetite and a buoyant spirit. After his dinner and a cigarette, he sat steadily down to work, determined not to let anything disturb him, for he remembered his promise to the doctor, and made up his mind to make the best of the time at his disposal.

For an hour or so he worked all right, and then his thoughts began to wander from his books. The actual circumstances around him, the calls on his physical attention, and his nervous susceptibility were not to be denied. By this time the wind had become a gale, and the gale a storm. The old house, solid though it was, seemed to shake to its foundations, and the storm roared and raged through its many chimneys and its queer old gables, producing strange, unearthly sounds in the empty rooms and corridors. Even the great alarm bell on the roof must have felt the force of the wind, for the rope rose and fell slightly, as though the bells were moved a little from time to time, and the limber rope fell on the oak floor with a hard and hollow sound.

As Malcolmson listened to it, he bethought himself of the doctor's words, 'It is the rope which the hangman used for the victims of the Judge's judicial rancour,' and he went over to the corner of the fireplace and took it in his hand to look at it. There seemed a sort of deadly interest in it, and as he stood there he lost himself for a moment in speculation as to who these victims were, and the grim wish of the Judge to have such a ghastly relic ever under his eyes. As he stood there, the swaying of the bell on the roof still lifted the rope now and again; but presently there came a new sensation—a sort of tremor in the rope, as though something was moving along it.

Looking up instinctively, Malcolmson saw the great rat coming slowly down towards him, glaring at him steadily. He dropped the rope and started back with a muttered curse, and the rat turning ran up the rope again and disappeared, and at the same instant Malcolmson became conscious that the noise of the rats, which had ceased for a while, began again.

All this set him thinking, and it occurred to him that he had not investigated the lair of the rat or looked at the pictures, as he had intended. He lit the other lamp without the shade, and, holding it up, went and stood opposite the third picture from the fireplace on the right-hand side where he had seen the rat disappear on the previous night.

At the first glance he started back so suddenly that he almost dropped the lamp, and a deadly pallor overspread his face. His knees shook, and heavy drops of sweat came on his forehead, and he trembled like an aspen. But he was young and plucky, and pulled himself together, and after the pause of a few seconds stepped forward again, raised the lamp, and examined the picture which had been dusted and washed, and now stood out clearly.

It was of a judge dressed in his robes of scarlet and ermine. His face was strong and merciless, evil, crafty, and vindictive, with a sensual mouth, hooked nose of ruddy colour, and shaped like the beak of a bird of prey. The rest of the face was of a cadaverous colour. The eyes were of peculiar brilliance and with a terribly malignant expression. As he looked at them, Malcolmson grew cold, for he saw there the very counterpart of the eyes of the great rat. The lamp almost fell from his hand as he saw the rat with its baleful eyes peering out through the hole in the corner of the picture, and noted the sudden cessation of the noise of the other rats. However, he pulled himself together, and went on with his examination of the picture.

The Judge was seated in a great high-backed carved oak chair, on the right-hand side of a great stone fireplace where, in the corner, a rope hung down from the ceiling, its end lying coiled on the floor. With a feeling of something like horror, Malcolmson recognised the scene of the room as it stood, and gazed around him in an awe-struck manner, as though he expected to find some strange presence behind him. Then he looked over to the corner of the fireplace—and with a loud cry he let the lamp fall from his hand.

There, in the Judge's arm-chair, with the rope hanging behind, sat the rat with the Judge's baleful eyes, now intensified and with a fiendish leer. Save for the howling of the storm without, there was silence.

The fallen lamp recalled Malcolmson to himself. Fortunately it was of metal, and so the oil was not spilt. However, the practical need of attending to it settled at once his nervous apprehensions. When he had turned it out, he wiped his brow and thought for a moment.

'This will not do,' he said to himself. 'If I go on like this I shall become a crazy fool. This must stop! I promised the Doctor I would not take tea. Faith, he was pretty right! My nerves must have been getting into a queer state. Funny I did not notice it. I never felt better in my life. However, it is all right now, and I shall not be such a fool again.'

Then he mixed himself a good stiff glass of brandy and water and resolutely sat down to his work.

It was nearly an hour when he looked up from his book, disturbed by the sudden stillness. Without, the wind howled and roared louder than ever, and the rain drove in sheets against the windows, beating like hail on the glass; but within there was no sound whatever, save the echo of the wind as it roared in the great chimney, and now and then a hiss as a few raindrops found their way down the chimney in a lull of the storm. The fire had fallen low and had ceased to flame, though it threw out a red glow. Malcolmson listened attentively, and presently heard a thin, squeaking noise, very faint. It came from the corner of the room where the rope hung down, and he thought it was the creaking of the rope on the floor as the swaying of the bell raised and lowered it. Looking up, however, he saw in the dim light the great rat clinging to the rope and gnawing it. The rope was already nearly gnawed through—he could see the lighter colour where the strands were laid bare. As he looked, the job was completed, and the severed end of the rope fell clattering on the oaken floor, whilst for an instant the great rat remained like a knob or tassel at the end of the rope, which now began to sway to and fro. Malcolmson felt for a moment another pang of terror as he thought that now the possibility of calling the outer world to his assistance was cut off, but an intense anger took its place, and seizing the book he was reading he hurled it at the rat. The blow was well aimed, but before the missile could reach it, the rat dropped off and struck the floor with a soft thud. Malcolmson instantly rushed over towards it, but it darted away and disappeared in the darkness of the shadows of the room. Malcolmson felt that his work was over for the night, and determined then and there to vary the monotony of the proceedings by a hunt for the rat, and took off the green shade of the lamp so as to insure a wider spreading light. As he did so, the gloom of the upper part of the room was relieved, and in the new flood of light, great by comparison with the previous darkness, the pictures on the wall stood out boldly. From where he stood, Malcolmson saw right opposite to him the third picture on the wall from the right of the fireplace. He rubbed his eyes in surprise, and then a great fear began to come upon him.

In the centre of the picture was a great irregular patch of brown canvas, as fresh as when it was stretched on the frame. The background was as before, with chair and chimney-corner and rope, but the figure of the Judge had disappeared.

Malcolmson, almost in a chill of horror, turned slowly round, and then he began to shake and tremble like a man in a palsy.

His strength seemed to have left him, and he was incapable of action or movement, hardly even of thought. He could only see and hear.

There, on the great high-backed carved oak chair sat the Judge in his robes of scarlet and ermine, with his baleful eyes glaring vindictively, and a smile of triumph on the resolute, cruel mouth, as he lifted with his hands a *black cap*. Malcolmson felt as if the blood was running from his heart, as one does in moments of prolonged suspense. There was a singing in his ears. Without, he could hear the roar and howl of the tempest, and through it, swept on the storm, came the striking of midnight by the great chimes in the marketplace. He stood for a space of time that seemed to him endless, still as a statue and with wide-open, horror-struck eyes, breathless. As the clock struck, so the smile of triumph on the Judge's face intensified, and at the last stroke of midnight, he placed the black cap on his head.

Slowly and deliberately the Judge rose from his chair and picked up the piece of the rope of the alarm bell which lay on the floor, drew it through his hands, as if he enjoyed its touch, and then deliberately began to knot one end of it, fashioning it into a noose. This he tightened and tested with his foot, pulling hard at it till he was satisfied, and then making a running noose of it, which he held in his hand. Then he began to move along the table on the opposite side to Malcolmson, keeping his eyes on him until he had passed him, when with a quick movement he stood in front of the door. Malcolmson then began to feel that he was trapped and tried to think of what he should do. There was some fascination in the Judge's eyes, which he never took off him, and he had, perforce, to look. He saw the Judge approach—still keeping between him and the door—and raise the noose and throw it towards him as if to entangle him. With a great effort he made a quick movement to one side, and saw the rope fall beside him, and heard it strike the oaken floor. Again the Judge raised the noose and tried to ensnare him, ever keeping his baleful eyes fixed on him, and each time by a mighty effort the student just managed to evade it. So this went on for many times, the Judge seeming never discouraged nor discomposed at failure, but playing as a cat does with a mouse. At last in despair, which had reached its climax, Malcolmson cast a quick glance round him. The lamp seemed to have blazed up, and there was a fairly good light in the room. At the many rat-holes and in the chinks and crannies of the wainscot he saw the rats' eyes; and this aspect, that was purely physical, gave him a gleam of comfort. He looked around and saw that the rope of the great alarm bell was laden with rats. Every inch of it was covered with them, and more and more were pouring through the small circular hole in the ceiling whence it emerged, so that with their weight the bell was beginning to sway.

Hark! it had swayed till the clapper had touched the bell. The sound was but a tiny one but the bell was only beginning to sway, and it would increase.

At the sound, the Judge, who had been keeping his eyes fixed on Malcolmson, looked up, and a scowl of diabolical anger overspread his face. His eyes fairly glowed like hot coals, and he stamped his foot with a sound that seemed to make the house shake. A dreadful peal of thunder broke overhead as he raised the rope again, whilst the rats kept running up and down the rope as though working against time. This time, instead of throwing it, he drew close to his victim, and held open the noose as he approached. As he came closer, there seemed something paralysing in his very presence, and Malcolmson stood rigid as a corpse. He felt the Judge's icy fingers touch his throat as he adjusted the rope. The noose tightened—tightened. Then the Judge, taking the rigid form of the student in his arms, carried him over and placed him standing in the oak chair, and stepping up beside him, put his hand up and caught the end of the swaying rope of the alarm bell. As he raised his hand, the rats fled squeaking and disappeared through the hole in the ceiling. Taking the end of the noose which was round Malcolmson's neck, he tied it to the hanging bell-rope, and then descending pulled away the chair.

When the alarm bell of the Judge's House began to sound, a crowd soon assembled. Lights and torches of various kinds appeared, and soon a silent crowd was hurrying to the spot. They knocked loudly at the door, but there was no reply. Then they burst in the door and poured into the great dining-room, the doctor at the head.

There at the end of the rope of the great alarm bell hung the body of the student, and on the face of the Judge in the picture was a malignant smile.

The *Werewolf*

C.A. Kincaid

It was a terribly hot afternoon in July, some fifty years ago, in Upper Sind. In the Deccan, cooling showers had turned the hard earth, baked by the summer winds, into a perfect paradise. The soil there was bright with long green grass. The hills rose emerald to the sky, although their summits were often veiled by the monsoon mists; and delightful breezes swept over the glad earth to the great joy of foreign sojourners in the Indian plateau. Even in the Punjab and the Gangetic valley, heavy rain had fallen, and if the air seemed stuffy to the traveller from southern India, his eyes rejoiced in the rich foliage and endless maize fields, while his ears listened joyfully to the murmuring sound of new-born streams, as they tinkled and splashed on their way to join the brimming rivers.

In Upper Sind, the landscape was quite different. Rain hardly ever falls there except in the cold weather, and while more favoured parts of India revel in the monsoon, none of it reaches that strange land. Irrigated by canals from the Indus, the fields are in winter gay with young wheat, and he who visits Upper Sind in January may well think that he has reached some heavenly spot. But let him go there in July or August and he will soon change his opinion. All day long the hot wind roars, driving the mercury up to 120° in the shade; nor is there much relief at night. The hot wind drops, but the thermometer still marks over a hundred; the sandflies and mosquitoes buzz all night, and moonbeams like the rays of a powerful electric headlight pour down on the would-be sleeper's face, making slumbering exceedingly difficult.

In the middle of this sunsplashed region is Sehwan, formerly an important town, but now greatly sunk in importance. One thing it still claims with justice is that it is one of the hottest places on earth. A Persian poet once in the bitterness of his heart asked the Almighty why, after making Sehwan and Sibi, he thought it worthwhile to make Hell. The afternoon on which this story opens was well worthy of Sehwan's ancient reputation. The train steamed slowly into Sehwan station from Sukkur. The railway on the left bank of the Indus had not then been built, so the railtrack passed through Sehwan on its way to Karachi and the seacoast. The last carriage on the train was the saloon of the Traffic Superintendent. It was far roomier than the ordinary first class carriages, as befitted the quarters of a senior railway official; but nothing could keep out the heat or make the interior cool. The shutters were closed. A railway coolie pulled a diminutive punka fixed on the roof, but he merely stirred into motion the heavy, hot air. There were two occupants of the saloon; one was the Traffic Superintendent, Frank Bollinger; the other was a Major Sinclair, whom he had known for some years. He had invited his friend to share the saloon instead of sweltering in the first class compartment and sharing it with two missionaries, their wives and babies.

'I shall be devoutly thankful,' said Bollinger, 'when we get out of this Hell into the monsoon area.'

'When will that be?'

'Once we pass the Lakhi gorge it will be better. They say the monsoon dies there and so they call the gorge the gate of Hell. It is true that once past that frightful mass of heated limestone, one does begin to feel a breath of cooler air. It gradually grows in strength; so we ought to get a good night on our way to Karachi.'

'I am very glad to hear that. I could not sleep a wink in this part of the world, could you?'

'Oh! I have had such a long experience of hot nights that I might; but thank God! there will be no need to make the experiment.'

Just then, the train drew up in Sehwan station. The station master, Isarmal, who had known Bollinger in earlier days, came running up to pay his respects. His face beamed all over with the pleasure that an Indian almost always feels at meeting a former English friend. Bollinger remembered well the little station master and was also very glad to see him and have a chat over old times.

To let the two old acquaintances have their talk out, Major Sinclair got out of the carriage and strolled about on the platform. After Bollinger and Isarmal had been gossiping together for about a quarter of an hour, the former said suddenly:

'I say, Mr Isarmal, why are we staying here so long? I never remember waiting more than five minutes at Sehwan before.'

'I am afraid, Sir—I am very sorry, Sir—the river has breached the line some four miles down and the train cannot go on until tomorrow morning.'

'Do you mean to say that we shall have to stay all night in this inferno? I am afraid, the Major Sahib will not like that at all. He was grumbling at the heat when the train was moving; what he'll say when he hears that we will have to pass the night in a stationary train, I can't think. He will swear horribly.'

'Yes indeed, Sir,' said Mr Isarmal, anxious to agree to everything his English friend said, 'the Major Sahib will swear horribly.'

Just then all doubts were settled by the arrival of Sinclair in a frightful temper. After so varied an outburst of blasphemy that it filled Bollinger with respectful awe, he shouted:

'Damn it all, Bollinger, have you heard that we have to spend the night in this hellhole?'

'Yes; I'm awfully sorry, old chap; but it cannot be helped. The Indus is in flood and it is just as capricious as a spoilt harlot. Still, it will only be for one night and you'll be able to wipe out your arrears of sleep, when we near Karachi.'

'My dear chap, I'm not going to sleep in your saloon. I have just been talking to the khansama of the rest-house. He says it is up on the top of a hill and all night one gets a cool breeze from the river. He'll give us dinner and he'll call us at six a.m. so that we shan't miss the train. He'll put our beds out in the open and he swears that we'll be able to sleep like tops.'

Just then the khansama himself came up. He was a powerfully built Panjabi Musulman with a long black beard and very strange yellow eyes. His face in repose had a villainous expression. He had a smile that rarely came off, but it was a very unpleasant one;

it was rather like the smile of a savage Alsatian fawning on its master. He could speak a little broken English, which in the case of poor linguists like Major Sinclair was a great attraction. On reaching the saloon he stood at the door and addressing Bollinger very deferentially, said:

'The Major Sahib, he coming to resthouse. Sahib, please come, too, and have good night in cool breeze. I give good dinner and you get good sleep and I wake you six a.m. Madras time. Down here too dammed hot, you get no sleep at all, Sahib.'

Bollinger could not help thinking of the old nursery rhyme 'Won't you walk into my parlour said the spider to the fly' and anyway he had no wish to leave his comfortable saloon and a dinner served by his own servants for a hard bed and a doubtful meal at a rest-house half a mile away. He politely thanked the khansama.

'No, Khansama; I shall be quite all right here. It may be hot, but I doubt whether it will be any cooler on the top of your Himalayan peak. After all, I have been there and it is only about thirty feet high and my dinner will be better than any you can give me.'

The khansama's yellow eyes flashed disagreeably, but he continued as before to smile in his canine way and to repeat mechanically:

'Sahib, I give you very good dinner. A cool breeze will blow all night. You get good sleep and to-morrow I call you at six a.m. Madras time.'

At last, Bollinger said impatiently: 'It's no use going on jabbering like that. I'm just not going to your rest-house. I'm going to stay here and there's an end of it.'

Suddenly, Sinclair broke in: 'Well, I'm not. I'm damned if I'm going to spend the night in your sardine box.' Turning to his butler, he said: 'Here, boy, get my luggage out of the saloon and put it in a tonga and tell the man to drive to the rest-house. You can come with the khansama in another.'

Bollinger, taken aback, replied with stiff courtesy: 'My dear Sinclair, you must, of course, please yourself. I shall stay in the old sardine box and you'll have a good dinner and a capital night. Goodnight!'

The Major, without troubling to answer, walked off with the khansama and Bollinger resumed his talk with Mr Isarmal, the station master.

When the khansama and Sinclair had passed out of sight, Isarmal suddenly said in a low earnest voice: 'Thank God, you did not go, Sahib, with that terrible man. If you had you would be as good as dead already. The Major Sahib will not be alive tomorrow.'

'What on earth are you talking about, Isarmal?'

'It is that khansama, sir. He is not really a man, but a—a—a—I have forgotten the English word; we call it in Sindi a *lakhibaghar*.'

'A hyena, you mean,' said Bollinger, who knew some Sindi.

'Yes, Sahib, he turns himself every night into a hyena and eats anyone whom he finds sleeping alone on a cot in the open. We say that he is the reincarnation of a horrible man called Anu Kasai.'

'Oh, you mean that fellow who ate up Bodlo Bahar?'

'Yes, I see the Sahib knows the story. Bodlo Bahar was the disciple of our great Sehwan saint Lal Shabaz. One day he disappeared. The following morning one of the saint's disciples saw that the bits of mutton that he was cooking for his dinner were jumping about strangely in his pot. Other disciples had the same tale to tell. So, Lal Shahbaz said: "It must be our Bodlo Bahar," and went to the Governor of Sehwan. He asked from whom they had bought the mutton. They all said, "From the butcher Anu Kasai." Now, this wicked man had once been very prosperous, but he had fallen on evil days; and having no money to buy sheep, he used to murder strangers and sell their flesh as mutton. The Governor arrested Anu Kasai and searched his shop and house. They were full of human bones. He had for months escaped punishment, but he was caught when he killed a saint like Bodlo Bahar.'

'How did the Governor punish him?'

'He walled him up in the battlements of Sehwan fort, that is the hill on which the rest-house now stands. As you pass it you can see a sort of hollow in the side of it. That is where they walled up Anu the butcher.'

'But what is this talk of the khansama being his reincarnation?'

'Well, Sahib, he has only been here three or four months and yet several people in the town have disappeared. Whenever they have done so, a large hyena has been seen galloping through Sehwan. Not only that, but two Chota Sahibs (subordinate Europeans) who went to the rest-house have also disappeared. The khansama said the same in both cases. They dined and slept outside the rest-house, but when he brought the tea next morning they had vanished. We say the khansama turns himself into a hyena and eats them during the night. You will never see the Major Sahib again, I am afraid; but thank God you are here! Still, at night close the doors and windows of your saloon, otherwise that khansama may attack you even here. We always shut ourselves in at night, although it is so hot.'

Bollinger was far too wise to laugh at the station master's story. He did not believe that the khansama and the hyena were the same: but remembering his villainous expression he did think it possible that he was a murderer; and after Isarmal had left, he began to wonder what he should do.

At last, he determined to go to the rest-house and share the danger, if any, with Sinclair. He had no gun, but he had a long heavy hunting knife that, had it been a bit sharper, would have been a very efficient weapon. He did not bother to take his servant as he did not wish to have him on his hands, too. In the glare of the setting sun he walked alone along the dusty limestone road and then up the steep side of the old fort, now the rest-house. He noticed, as he walked, a depression in the fort wall and said to himself that that must be the place where they walled up Anu Kasai. At last, he reached the top of the old fort. It formed a plateau and in the centre was the rest-house. He arrived just as Sinclair was sitting down to dinner outside the building. It certainly was far cooler than in the station siding, for a cool breeze blew from the river.

'Come along, Bollinger, I am so glad you have come,' said Sinclair cordially. 'You must dine with me. We can get a good night here in the breeze. I say, I'm awfully sorry for having been so grumpy just now. I cannot make out what came over me.'

'Oh, that's all right!' said Bollinger cheerily, wondering secretly what Sinclair would think of Isarmal's tale. The khansama also welcomed Bollinger and made ready a place for him. He then served an excellent dinner and after dinner began to put the two officers' cots outside.

'Oh, don't do that, we shall sleep inside.'

'It will be damned hot, almost as hot as in your saloon below.'

'Oh no, we shall leave the windows open and so get a through draught. The station master tells me that the place is alive with scorpions and that one may well get stung if one sleeps outside.'

Sinclair looked towards the khansama, but he made no objection, so Sinclair said, 'Very well; but it will be so hot that we shall not get a wink of sleep.'

'Oh well, no matter, we'll play picquet until midnight. After that it will cool down sufficiently for us to sleep indoors."

'Right-o!' said Sinclair gloomily, wishing Bollinger in the infernal regions.

From nine on, the two men played cards and Bollinger deliberately played badly so that Sinclair might win and remain interested in the game. The simple device succeeded and Sinclair was so pleased that at 11 p.m. he was still absorbed in the picquet. Just then, someone tried the door, but Bollinger had bolted it. A few seconds later, the khansama appeared at the window in front of which had been fixed wire netting to keep the numerous pigeons from soiling the rooms.

'I have brought iced lemonade for the Sahibs,' said the khansama with an obsequious grin. Bollinger thought that he had never seen any man with such an odious expression, and his yellow eyes were twinkling, as if with some horrible anticipation.

'All right,' said Sinclair. 'I'll open the door.' He rose, and before Bollinger could stop him he had drawn the bolt. Bollinger pushed him aside and flung his weight against the door. It was too late. A huge paw and the muzzle of a monstrous hyena forced their way through the opening. Bollinger brought his knife down with all his strength on the paw. It was too blunt to cut deeply through the hair, but the blow was a heavy one and numbed the brute's limb. A bloodcurdling growl followed and the paw and snout were withdrawn. Bollinger slammed the door and shot the bolt.

'Thank God, we got the better of that brute. I fancy we're rid of it for the night!'

Hearing a noise he looked round and cried 'By God! we're not!' Through a gap in the netting of one of the windows the hyena had forced its head and in a few seconds would have been in the room. This time, Bollinger decided to use the point and not the edge of his knife. He made a thrust at the brute's throat. It swung its head aside in time to avoid a fatal stab; nevertheless, the knife scored a deep cut in its neck. It gave another bloodcurdling growl, dragged out its head and, with blood streaming from its wound, it raced off laughing in the diabolical way that hyenas do when hurt.

'By Jove! What an escape!' said Sinclair thankfully; 'but I suppose you fight that sort of brute everyday.'

'No, thank Heaven, I don't,' and then Bollinger told Sinclair the station master's story and how, on hearing it, he had come to the rest-house to see if his help was needed.

Sinclair went up to Bollinger and shook him cordially by the hand: 'Then, my dear chap, I owe you my life. I cannot say how grateful I feel. I shall never forget your help.'

The other smiled and said: 'Oh, nonsense! You'd have done the same for me. But, I say, didn't you bring your boy with you?'

'Yes, I did. I wonder where he is. I hope to goodness the khansama has not killed him.'

'Well, we had better go and look but we must be very wary, for if the hyena killed your boy, he'll come back.'

'All right, come along. You've got a knife, haven't you? I'am afraid I've got nothing.'

The two men went to the back of the rest-house and there they found below a slight slope the dead body of Sinclair's Goanese servant. His throat was completely torn open. The hyena must have crept up noiselessly to the servant's bed and torn out his throat, killing him instantly. Then, it must have again become the khansama and tried to enter the rest-house with the iced lemonade.

Sinclair stood sorrowfully by the dead man, who had been many years in his service and to whom he was greatly attached.

'I say, we can't do anything for the poor chap,' said Bollinger, 'so we had better go straight back to the rest-house. I have a horrid feeling that the brute is somewhere near, coming back to its kill. By God! there it is!'

He pointed to where a huge striped form was galloping straight for them. The two men ran for the rest-house as fast as they could; they only reached it in time through Bollinger throwing his coat at the brute's head and thus gaining a moment's respite.

'I wonder what it will do now,' said Sinclair, but it did nothing. It went slowly back to the body of the Goanese and began to crunch it up, every now and then breaking into screams of diabolical laughter when its neck hurt it.

'I wish to God I had a gun', said Bollinger, 'but as we haven't, let's try to get some sleep. One will sit up and watch while the other lies down. I'll sit up first.'

'All right,' said Sinclair, and lying down on one of the cots fell dead asleep in spite of the heat and his servant's death.

Bollinger sat in a chair and tried as best he could to keep awake. Still, he must have dropped off for a minute or so, for waking up with a start he saw in the bright moonlight the baleful glare of the hyena's eyes as it stared at him through the wire netting. He drew his knife and ran with a shout towards the netting, but the hyena with a growl of fury jumped back and galloped off.

Sinclair woke and hearing what had happened said: 'We must both sit up, otherwise the brute will return and get us.'

The two friends sat and smoked and talked through the weary hours until about 5:30 a.m. when their troubles came to an end. A crowd of Sindis, led by Isarmal, came to the rest-house to see what had happened to the two Englishmen.

'God be praised!' exclaimed Isarmal earnestly. 'Nothing has happened and you are both safe!'

'We are safe, but look at this,' and Bollinger led the crowd of Sindis to the half-eaten remains of the unfortunate Goanese: 'The khansama killed him!'

Isarmal's face grew grim, and turning to the rest of the crowd he cried: 'Brothers, we are Sindis. The khansama is a Panjabi and therefore of a race that we hate. He is clearly the reincarnation of Anu Kasai. When the train has gone we must deal with him.'

The two Englishmen walked back with Isarmal to the station, where the train was standing; as they walked, Bollinger related the events of the night. Afterwards, Isarmal repeated the story in Sindi to the men following him. On reaching the saloon nothing more was said. The two weary travellers got in and Isarmal, as he waved on the train, turned to the Sindis, who were mostly Musulmans, and cried: 'The Sahibs are safe, *Alhamdalilla* (God be praised)!'

After a hot, slow journey, the Englishmen reached Karachi. On the way Bollinger said: 'I fancy the khansama has had a bad quarter of an hour. He is a Panjabi and, as Isarmal said, of a race hated by the Sindis.'

'But why do the Sindis hate the Panjabis? I like them.'

'I really do not quite know. Perhaps, like French and Germans, Sindis and Panjabis live too near together. The Panjabis, too, are bigger men as a rule than the Sindis and they throw their weight about. The Sindis seem very much afraid of them. Indeed I remember hearing a Sindi proverb that says: "If one Panjabi comes, sit still and say nothing. If two come, then pack up your kit at once, abandon your house and clear out." Anyway, Panjabis are not liked in these parts.'

'They don't seem to be!'

Two mornings after their arrival, Davidson, the District Superintendent of Police, burst unceremoniously into Bollinger's bungalow and onto the verandah, where he was having his *chota hazri* or morning tea.

'I'm sorry, Bollinger, but I must see you. I have just received an official report from the Chief Constable of Sehwan to the effect that the villagers, led by the station master, broke into the khansama's house, dragged him out, although he was very ill, and walled him into the battlements of the old fort. He hints that you know something about it. In the meantime, he has arrested the station master, Isarmal I think he calls him.'

'Half a mo', Davidson! I fancy I have a letter from the station master in my morning post. I'll open it.' Tearing open the envelope, Bollinger read aloud the following note, very short and quaintly expressed:

Honoured Sir,

The Chief Constable of Sehwan, who is a Panjabi, is troubling us because of the death of that Anu Kasai, the khansama. After Your Honour's departure we went to his house and found him very ill from a severe wound in the throat. We found in his house the property of the two missing Chota Sahibs; seeing this he became very obstinate and refused to answer our questions. Very soon he died. When dead, we put him where Anu Kasai was walled up. The Sahib knows the facts and will kindly do the needful.

'Well, Bollinger, he says you know the facts, for goodness sake let me have them.'

Bollinger told the full story of the adventure and Sinclair supported him in every detail. Still, as told in an Englishman's house in Karachi, it did not sound very convincing.

'Hang it all, Bollinger!' You can't expect me to believe this tale of a werewolf.

'Well, Isarmal says that they found in the khansama's house the property of those two missing subordinates. That raises a presumption that he is a murderer, anyway.'

'The Chief Constable says nothing about that.'

'He is a brother Panjabi and can scarcely be expected to. Look here, instead of arguing, let's go off and call on the Commissioner. He is the Inspector-General of Police, as well as of everything else and we'll abide by his orders.'

'Right-o!' said the District Superintendent and at 11 a.m. all three men met to call on Government House.

The Commissioner was a big genial man, who combined with a very cordial manner a vast amount of commonsense. He greeted all three men pleasantly. Then, he turned to the D.S.P. who was in uniform:

'Well, Davidson, what's the trouble?'

'I think, Sir, Bollinger had better tell you his yarn first and then I'll supplement it with my information.'

'Capital! Go ahead, Bollinger.'

The railwayman repeated his story and Sinclair confirmed it. Then, Davidson shewed the Commissioner his Chief Constable's report and Bollinger produced Isarmal's letter.

The Commissioner's keen intellect grasped immediately all the facts and came at once to a decision.

'Look here, Bollinger, you can't expect me to accept as gospel your story of the werewolf or werehyena; but the khansama seems to have been a murderer all right. The discovery in his house of the property of the two subordinates points to that. I have often been worried as to what became of them. Again, I do not see why we should not believe Isarmal's statement that they did not wall in the khansama until he was dead. Anyway, it will be impossible to disprove it; for all the eye-witnesses will support Isarmal. In any case, if you go into the witness box, Bollinger, and tell your adventure with the khansama-cum-hyena, my administration will be the laughing stock of all India. Think how the young lions of the *Pioneer* will sharpen their wit at our expense. No! No, we must stop the prosecution at all costs. Look here, Davidson, you wire to the Chief Constable to drop the case and release Isarmal and any others he may have arrested. I shall myself transfer to some other district the Chief Constable; for he seems to have been very slack over the disappearance of the two subordinates. Well, good morning.'

Isarmal was duly released and resumed his duties as station master. But Bollinger did not forget him. Using his influence with the railway chiefs, he got Isarmal first promoted to be station master of Radhan and then of Sukkur, a very important post. This

Isarmal retained until his retirement. He lived for many years on an ample pension and nothing gave him greater pleasure than to tell the story of the Panjabi who could turn himself into a hyena and how he nearly ate up the two Sahibs. He gave ample credit to Bollinger Sahib for his courage and resource; but the person for whom he reserved the fullest commendation was none other than Mr Isarmal, late station master of Sukkur.

Jeremy and the Runaways*

Hugh Walpole

[*Jeremy Cole, on returning to Thompson's School, found that he had been changed to a new dormitory. It was a distinction to be there, a move-up in the school world, his companions being two older boys—the chums Pug Raikes and Stokesley Maj. The latest plot is for he and Raikes to run away—to go to sea after 'a week, a fortnight, a month in London at the very finest hotels, with heaps to eat and drink, and theatres every night.'*]

Later in the day, Raikes took him into a corner of the playground and whispered dramatically:

'We're going to do it. It's all settled.'

'Oh!' gasped Jeremy.

'It's to be next Sunday. You're right about not coming. You're too young.' Raikes sounded very old indeed as he said this. 'You swear you won't tell a living soul?'

---

*From *Jeremy and Hamlet*.

'Of course I won't.'

'You'll swear by God Almighty?'

'I swear by God Almighty.'

'Never to breathe a word to any boy, master or animal?'

'Never to breathe a word to any boy, master or animal.'

'You're a good sort, Stocky. Somehow one can trust you—and one can't most of them. They'll be on to you after we're gone, you know!'

'I don't care.'

'They'll try to get it out of you.'

'I don't care. They shan't.'

'In any way they can. Perhaps they'll stop your football.'

Jeremy drew a deep breath. 'I don't care,' he repeated slowly.

'We'll have a great time,' Raikes said, as though addressing his reluctant half. 'We'll come back ever so rich in a year or two, and then won't you wish you'd come with us!'

What Jeremy did wish was that they had told him nothing about it. Oh, how he wished it! Why had they dragged him in? Suppose they *did* stop his football? Oh, but they couldn't! It wasn't his fault that he'd heard about it.

'Look here, Raikes,' he said, 'don't you tell me any more. I don't want to know anything about it. ... Then they can't come on me afterwards.'

'That's sound,' said Raikes. 'All right; we won't.'

The days, then, that intervened before Sunday could have only one motive. It seemed incredible to Jeremy that the two conspirators should appear now so ordinary; they should have had in some way a flaring mark, a scarlet letter, to set them aside from the rest of mankind. Not at all. They followed their accustomed duties, ate their meals, did their impositions, played their games just as they had always done.

Even at night, when they were left alone in the dormitory, they spoke very little about it. Jeremy was outside it now, and although they trusted him, 'one never knew', and they were not going to give anything away.

The great Sunday came, a day of blazing autumnal gold, enough breeze to stir the leaves and send them like ragged scraps of brown paper lazily through the air. The Sunday bells came like challenges to guilty consciences upon the misty sky. Jeremy did not see the two of them after breakfast. Indeed, in the strange way that these terrific events have of suddenly slipping for half an hour from one's consciousness, during morning chapel he forgot about the whole affair, and stared half asleep through the long chapel window out into the purple field, wondering about a thousand little things—some lines he had to write, a pot of jam that he was going to open that night at tea for the first time, and how Hamlet was in Polchester and what, just then, he would be doing.

He went on his accustomed Sunday walk with Riley, and it was only when they were hurrying back over the leaf-thickened paths towards a sun like a red orange that he suddenly remembered. Why, at this very moment they would be making for the station! He stopped in the path.

'By gum!' he said.

'What is it?' asked Riley. 'Been stung by a bee?'

'No; just thought of something.'

'You *do* look queer!'

'It's nothing.' He moved on. It seemed impossible that the woods should stay just as they were, unmoved by this great event, hanging like old coloured tapestry with their thin dead leaves between the black poles of trees. Unmoved! No one knew. No one but himself.

The great moment came when in chapel, looking across to the other side, he saw that their places were empty. Nothing much in that for the ordinary world—fellows were often late for chapel—but for him it meant everything. The deed was positively accomplished. They must be actually at this moment in the train, and he was the only creature in the whole school who knew where they were.

Call-over followed chapel. He heard the names called. 'Stokesley!' and then, more impatiently, after a little pause, 'Stokesley!' again. Then 'Raikes!' and, after a moment, 'Raikes!' again. Nothing, after that, happened for an hour. Then call-over once more at supper. Raikes and Stokesley again called and again absent.

Five minutes after supper the school sergeant came for him.

'Mr Thompson to see you in his study at once!'

Jeremy went.

Thompson was walking about, and very worried he looked. He had been talking to the matron and wheeled round when Jeremy came in.

'Ah, Cole. ... Leave us for a moment, matron, please.'

They were alone. Jeremy felt terribly small, shrivelled to nothing at all. He shuffled his feet and looked anywhere but at Thompson's anxious eyes. He liked Thompson and was aware, with a sudden flash, that this was more than a mere game—that it might be desperately serious for someone.

'Come here, Cole. I want you to keep this to yourself. Not to say a word to anyone, do you understand?'

'Yes, sir.'

'Good. It seems that Stokesley and Raikes have run away. They were neither at chapel nor at supper. Some of their things are missing. Now, you're the only other boy in their dormitory. Do you know anything at all about this?'

'No, sir.'

'Nothing?'

'No, sir.'

'They said nothing at all to you about this going?'

'No, sir.'

'Gave you no idea that they were thinking of it?'

'No, sir.'

Thompson paused, looked out of the window, walked up and down the room a little, then said:

'I make it a rule always to believe what any boy tells me. I've never found you untruthful, Cole. I don't say that you're not telling the truth now, but I know what your boys' code is. You mustn't sneak about another boy whatever happens. That's a code that has something to be said for it. It happens to have nothing to be said for it just now. You're young, and I don't expect you realise what this means. It involves many people beside themselves—their fathers and mothers and everyone in this school. You may be doing a very serious thing that will affect many people's lives if you don't tell me what you know. Do you realise that?'

'Yes, sir.'

'Well, then, did they say anything at all about going away?'

'No, sir.'

'Nothing at all to you?'

'No, sir.'

'Very well. You may go.'

Jeremy went. Outside he found the school in a ferment. Everyone knew. Stokesley and Raikes had run away. He was surrounded by a mob. They pressed in upon him from every side—big boys, little boys, old boys, young boys—everyone.

'Stocky! Where have they gone to? What did Thompson say to you? Did he whack you? Is he going to? Is it true that they've stolen a lot of the matron's money? What did they tell you? ... Oh, rot! Of course you know? Where have they gone to, Stocky? We'll give you the most awful hiding if you don't say. Come on, Stocky, out with it! When did they go? Just before chapel? Is Thompson awfully sick?'

But Jeremy stood his ground. He knew nothing at all. Nothing at all. They had said nothing to him.

During the four days that followed the characters, bodies and souls of the fugitives swelled into epic proportions. Four days in such circumstances can, at a small school, resemble centuries of time. No one thought or discussed anything but this, and there was not a boy in the place, from the eldest to the youngest, but envied those two passionately and would have given a year of holiday to be with them.

On Monday Mr Thompson went up to London. The rumours that sprang to life were marvellous. Stokesley had been seen at a theatre in London, and had been chased all the way down the Strand by an enormous crowd. Raikes had struck a policeman, and been put in a cell. They had been to Buckingham Palace and interviewed Her Majesty. They had started on a slaver for the South Seas. They had taken up jobs as waiters in a London restaurant.

To Jeremy these days were torture. In the first place he was dazzled by their splendour. Why had he been such a fool as to refuse to go with them? One might die tomorrow. Here was his great adventure offered to him, and he had rejected it.

As the tales circulated round him the atmosphere became more and more romantic. He forgot the real Stokesley and saw no longer the genuine Raikes. It no longer occurred to him that Stokesley had warts; he refused to see that so familiar picture of Raikes washing himself in the morning, trickling the cold water over his head, his two large ears, projecting, crimson. Clothed in gold and silver, they swung dazzling through the air, rosy clouds supporting them, to the haven where they would be—the haven of the South Seas, with gleaming, glittering sands, blue waters, monkeys in thousands, and pearls and diamonds for the asking.

Under these alluring visions even the football faded into grey monotony. In a practice game on Monday he played so badly that he expected to lose all chance of playing in the match at the end of the week; but, fortunately for him, everyone else played badly too. The mind of the school was in London, following the flight, the chase, the final escape—no time now for football or anything else.

The heroes that Stokesley and Raikes now were! Anyone who had an anecdote, however trivial, was listened to by admiring crowds. It was recalled how Stokesley, when a new boy, had endured the first tossing in the blanket with marvellous phlegm and indifference; how Raikes, when receiving a hamper from an affectionate aunt, had instantly distributed it round his table, so that almost at once there was none of it remaining. How Stokesley had once conducted a money-lending establishment with extraordinary force and daring for more than a fortnight; how Raikes had fought Bates Major, a boy almost twice his size, and had lasted into the sixth round—and so on.

Jeremy, of course, was affected by all this reminiscence, and himself recalled how, in the dormitory, Stokesley had said this clevèr thing, and Raikes had been on that occasion strangely daring. But behind this romance there was something more.

He was strangely and, as the hours advanced, quite desperately bothered by the question of his lie. In the first immediate instance of it he had not been bothered by it at all. When he had stood in Thompson's study it had not seemed to him a lie at all; so thickly clothed was he by his school convention that it had seemed the natural, the absolutely inevitable thing to do. His duty was not to give Stokesley and Raikes away, that was all.

But afterwards Thompson's troubled face came back to him, and that serious warning that perhaps, if he kept his knowledge back, the lives of hundreds of people might be affected. It was true that by the following morning everything that he knew was known by everyone else. The station-master from the junction came up after breakfast and gave information about the boys. He had thought it strange that they should be going up to London by themselves, but they had seemed so completely self-possessed that he had not liked simply on his own authority to stop them.

But had Jeremy told all that he knew on that first Sunday evening, many precious hours might have been gained and the fugitives caught at once. Alone in that little dormitory at night, the two empty beds staring at him, he had fallen into dreams, distressing, accusing nightmares. By Tuesday morning he was not at all sure that he was not a desperate criminal, worthy of prison and perhaps even of hanging.

He longed—how desperately he longed!—to discuss the matter with Riley. Riley was so full of wisdom and common sense and knew so much more than did Jeremy about life in general. But, having gone so far, he would not turn back, but he moved about on that Tuesday like Christian with his pack.

Then, on Tuesday evening, came the great news. They had been caught—they had given themselves up. They had spent all their money. Thompson was bringing them back with him on Wednesday morning.

The school waited breathlessly for the arrival. No one saw anything; only by midday it was whispered by everyone that they were there. By the afternoon it was known that they were shut away in the infirmary. No one was to see them or to speak to them.

During that morning how swiftly the atmosphere had changed! Only yesterday those two had been sailing for the South Seas; now, ostracised, waiting in horrible confinement for some terrible doom; they were only glorious, like one of Byron's heroes, in their 'damned prospects' and 'fatal overthrow'. All that day Jeremy thought of them, feeling in some unanalysed way as though he himself were responsible for their failure. Had he not done this, had he thought of that—and what would Thompson do?

At the end of breakfast next morning it was known. He made them a speech, speaking with a new gravity that even the smallest boy in the school (young Phipps, Junr., only about two feet high) could feel. He said that, as was by this time known to all of them, two of their number had run away, had spent several days in London, had been found, and brought back to the school. They would all understand how serious a crime this was, the unhappiness that it must have brought on the boys' parents, the harm that it might have done to the school itself. The boys were young; they had, apparently, no especial grievance with their school life, and they had done what they had from a silly, false sense of adventure rather than from any impulse of wickedness or desire for evil.

Nevertheless, they had wilfully made many people unhappy and broken laws upon whose preservation the very life of their school, that they all loved, depended. He was not sure that they had not done even more than that. He could not tell, of course, whether there were any boys in that room who had known of this before it occurred—he hoped from the bottom of his heart that no boy had told him an untruth; he knew that they had a code of their own, that whatever happened they were never to 'tell' about another boy. That code had its uses, but it could be carried too far. All the misery of these four days might have been spared had some boy given information at once. He would say no more about that. The boys had been given a choice between expulsion and a public flogging. They had both, without hesitation, chosen the flogging. The whole school was to be present that evening in Big Hall before first preparation.

Every seat in Big Hall was filled. The boys sat in classes, motionless, silent, not even an occasional whisper. The hissing of a furious gas-jet near the door was the only sound.

Jeremy would never forget that horrible half-hour. He was the criminal. He sat there, scarcely breathing, his eyes hot and dry, staring, although he did not know that he was staring, at the platform, empty save for a table and a chair, pressing his hands upon his knees, wishing that this awful thing might pass, thinking not especially of Stokesley or of Raikes, but of something that was himself and yet not himself, something that was pressed down into a dark hole and every tick of the school clock pressed him further. He saw the rows and rows of heads as though they had been the pattern of a carpet; and he was ashamed, desperately ashamed, as though he were standing up in front of them all naked.

The door behind the platform opened and Thompson came in. He was white and black and flat, like a drawing upon a sheet of paper. The gas gave a hysterical giggle at the sight of him. Behind him came Raikes and Stokesley, looking as they had always looked and yet quite different—actors playing a part. Behind them was the school sergeant, Crockett, a burly ex-sailorman, a friend of everyone when in a good temper. He looked sheepish now, shuffling on his feet. He looked terrible, too, because his coat was off and his sleeves rolled up, showing the ship and anchor tattoo that he showed as a favour to boys who had done their drill well.

Thompson came forward. He said:

'I don't want to prolong this, but you are all here because I wish you to remember this all your lives. I wish you to remember it, not because it is the punishment of two of your friends—indeed, it is my special wish that, as soon as it is over, you shall receive Stokesley and Raikes among you again as though nothing had occurred—but I want you all, from the youngest to the eldest to remember that there must be government, there must be rules, if men are to live in any sort of society together. We owe something to ourselves, we owe something to those who love us, we owe something to our country, and we owe something to our school. We cannot lead completely selfish lives—God does not mean us to do so. Our school is our friend. We belong to it, and we must be proud of it.'

He stepped back. The school sergeant came forward and whispered something to Stokesley. Stokesley himself undid his braces. His trousers fell down over his ankles. He bent forward over the table, hiding his face with his hands. Jeremy could not look. He felt sick; he wanted to cry. He heard the sound of the descending birch. One, two, three, four, five, six, seven—would it never end?—eight, nine, ten, eleven, twelve.

He heard the whole school draw a breath. Still he did not look. Stokesley had not made a sound.

There was a pause. Still he did not look. Now Raikes was there. The birch again. One, two, three, four—Then, as though someone were tearing the wall in two, a shrill cry: 'Oh! Oh!' ... Horrible—beastly. He was trembling from head to foot. He was low down in that hole now, and someone was pushing the earth in over his head. And now with the switch of the birch there was a low, monotonous sobbing, and then the sharp cry again that, at this second time, seemed to come from within Jeremy himself. Everything was dark. A longer pause, and the shuffling of feet. It was all over, and the boys were filing out. He raised his eyes to a world of crimson and flashing lights.

That night they were restored to their fellow-citizens. They were sitting on their beds in the Baby Dorm examining their wounds. Raikes could think of nothing but that he had cried. Stokesley consoled him. As a last word he said to Jeremy: 'Very decent of you, Stocky, not to give us away. We won't forget it, will we, Pug?'

'No, we won't,' said Pug, a naked, writhing figure, because he was trying to see his stripes.

'All the same,' said Stokesley, 'it was smart of you not to come. It was rotten; all of it. They were beastly to us at the hotel, and just took our money. We went to a rotten theatre; and it rained all the time, didn't it, Pug?'

'Beastly,' said Raikes.

The room was silent. So that was the end of the adventure. Jeremy, slipping off to sleep, suddenly loved the school, didn't want to leave it—no, never. Saw the rooms, one by one, the class-room, the dining-room, Big Hall—Thompson, the matron, Crockett. All warm and safe and cosy.

And London. Swimming in rain, chasing you, hating you, catching you up at the last with a birch.

Good old school—the end of *that* adventure.

Carnival on the Downs

GERALD KERSH

We are a queer people: I do not know what to make of us. Whatever anyone says for us is right; whatever anyone says against us is right. A conservative people, we would turn out our pockets for a rebel; and prim as we are, we love an eccentric.

We are an eccentric people. For example: we make a cult of cold baths—and of our lack of plumbing—and a boast of such characters as Dirty Dick of Bishopsgate, and Mr Lagg who is landlord of The White Swan at Wettendene.

Dirty Dick of Bishopsgate had a public house, and was a dandy, once upon a time. But it seems that on the eve of his marriage to a girl with whom he was in love he was jilted, with the wedding breakfast on the table. Thereafter, everything had, by his order, to be left exactly as it was on that fatal morning. The great cake crumbled, the linen mouldered, the silver turned black. The bar became filthy. Spiders spun their webs, which grew heavy and grey with insects and dirt. Dick never changed his wedding suit, nor his linen, either. His house became a byword for dirt and neglect... whereupon, he did good business there, and died rich.

Mr Lagg, who had a public house in Wettendene, which is in Sussex, seeing The Green Man redecorated and furnished with chromium chairs, capturing carriage trade, was at first discouraged. His house, The White Swan, attracted the local men who drank nothing but beer—on the profit of which, at that time, a publication could scarcely live.

Lagg grew depressed; neglected the house. Spiders spun their webs in the cellar, above and around the empty, mouldering barrels, hogsheads, kilderkins, nipperkins, casks and pins. He set up a bar in this odorous place—and so made his fortune. As the dirtiest place in Sussex, it became a meeting place for people who bathed every day. An American from New Orleans started the practice of pinning visiting cards to the beams. Soon, everybody who had a card pinned it up, so that Lagg's cellar was covered with them.

When he went to town, Lagg always came back with artificial spiders and beetles on springy wires, to hang from the low ceiling; also, old leather jacks, stuffed crocodiles and spiky rays from the Caribbean gulfs, and even a dried human head from the Amazon. Meanwhile, the cards accumulated, and so did the bills advertising local attractions—cattle shows, flower shows, theatricals, and what not.

And the despisers of what they called the 'great Unwashed' congregated there—the flickers-away of specks of dust—the ladies and gentlemen who could see a thumb print on a plate.

Why? Homesickness for the gutter, perhaps—it is an occupational disease of people who like strong perfumes.

I visited The White Swan, in passing, on holiday. The people in Wettendene called it—not without affection—The Mucky Duck. There was the usual vociferous gathering of long-toothed women in tight-cut tweeds, and ruddy men with two slits to their jackets, howling confidences, while old Lagg, looking like a half-peeled beetroot, brooded under the cobwebs.

He took notice of me when I offered him something to drink, and said: 'Stopping in Wettendene, sir?'

'Overnight,' I said. 'Anything doing?'

He did not care. 'There's the flower show,' he said, flapping about with a loose hand. 'There's the Christian Boys' Sports. All pinned up. Have a dekko. See for yourself.

So I looked about me.

That gentleman from New Orleans, who had pinned up the first card on the lowest bean, had started a kind of chain reaction. On the beams, the ceiling, and the very barrels, card jostled card, and advertisement jostled advertisement. I saw the card of the Duke of Chelsea overlapped by the large, red-pinned trade card of one George Grape, Rat-Catcher; a potato-crisp salesman's card half overlaid by that of the Hon. Iris Greene. The belly of a stuffed trout was covered with cards as an autumn valley with leaves.

But the great hogshead, it seemed, was set aside for the bills advertising local attractions. Many of these were out of date—for example, an advertisement of a Baby Show in 1932, another of a Cricket Match in 1934, and yet another for 'Sports' in 1923. As Mr Lagg had informed me, there were the printed announcements of the Christian Boys' affair and the Flower Show.

Under the Flower Show, which was scheduled for 14 August, was pinned a wretched little bill advertising, for the same fate, a 'Grand Carnival' in Wagnall's Barn on Long Meadow, Wettendene. Everything was covered with dust.

It is a wonderful place for dust. It is necessary, in The Mucky Duck cellar, to take your drink fast or clasp your hand over the top of the glass before it accumulates a grey scum or even a dead spider: the nobility and gentry like it that way. The gnarled old four-ale drinkers go to The Green Man: they have no taste for quaintness.

I knew nobody in Wettendene, and am shy of making new acquaintances. The 'Grand Carnival' was to begin at seven o'clock; entrance fee sixpence, children half price. It could not be much of a show, I reflected, at that price and in that place: a showman must be hard up, indeed, to hire a barn for his show in such a place. But I like carnivals and am interested in the people that follow them; so I set off at five o'clock.

Long Meadow is not hard to find: you go to the end of Wettendene High Street, turn sharp right at Scott's Corner where the village ends, and take the winding lane, Wettendene Way. This will lead you, through a green tunnel, to Long Meadow, where the big Wagnall's Barn is.

Long Meadow was rich grazing land in better times, but now it is good for nothing but a pitiful handful of sheep that nibble the coarse grass. There has been no use for the barn these last two generations. It was built to last hundreds of years; but the land died first. This had something to do with water—either a lack or an excess of it. Long Meadow is good for nothing much, at present, but the Barn stands firm and four-square to the capricious rains and insidious fogs of Wettendene Marsh. (If it were not for the engineers who dammed the river, the whole area would, by now, be under water.) However, the place is dry in dry weather.

Still, Long Meadow has the peculiarly dreary atmosphere of a swamp and Wagnall's Barn is incongruously sturdy in that wasteland. It is a long time since any produce was stocked in Wagnall's Barn. Mr Etheridge, who owns it, rents it for dances, amateur theatrical shows and what not.

That playbill aroused my curiosity. It was boldly printed in red, as follows:

!!! JOLLY JUMBO'S CARNIVAL !!!
!! THE ONE AND ONLY !!
COME AND SEE
!! GORGON, The Man Who Eats Bricks & Swallows Glass !!
!! THE HUMAN SKELETON !!
!! THE INDIA RUBBER BEAUTY –
She Can Put Her Legs Around Her Neck & Walk On Her Hands !!
!! A LIVE MERMAID !!
!! ALPHA, BETA, AND DOT.
The World–Famous Tumblers
With The Educated Dog !!
! JOLLY JUMBO !
!! JOLLY JUMBO !!

I left early, because I like to look behind the scenes, and have a chat with a wandering freak or two. I remembered a good friend of mine who had been a Human Skeleton—six foot six and weighed a hundred pounds—ate five meals a day, and was as strong as a bull. He told good stories in that coffee-bar that is set up where the Ringling Brothers and Barnum and Bailey Combined Circuses rest in Florida for the winter. I 'tasted sawdust', as the saying goes, and had a yearning to sit on the ground and hear strange stories. Not that I expected much of Wettendene. All the same the strangest people turn up at the unlikeliest places…

Then the rain came down, as it does in an English summer. The sky sagged, rumbled a borborygmic threat of thunderstorms, which seemed to tear open clouds like bags of water.

Knowing our English summer, I had come prepared with a mackintosh, which I put on as I ran for the shelter of the barn.

I was surprised to find it empty. The thunder was loud, now, and there were zigzags of lightning in the east; the pelting rain sounded on the meadow like a maraca. I took off my raincoat and lit a cigarette—and then, in the light of the match flame, I caught a glimpse of two red-and-green eyes watching me, in a far corner, about a foot away from the floor.

It was not yet night, but I felt in that moment such a pang of horror as comes only in the dark; but I am so constituted that, when frightened, I run forward. There was something unholy about Wagnall's Barn, but I should have been ashamed not to face it, whatever it might be. So I advanced, with my walking-stick; but then there came a most melancholy whimper, and I knew that the eyes belonged to a dog.

I made a caressing noise and said: 'Good dog, good doggie! Come on, doggie!'—feeling grateful for his company. By the light of another match, I saw a grey poodle, neatly clipped in the French style. When he saw me, he stood up on his hindlegs and danced.

In the light of that same match I saw, also, a man squatting on his haunches with his head in his hands. He was dressed only in trousers and a tattered shirt. Beside him lay a girl. He had made a bed for her out of his clothes and, the rain falling softer, I could hear her breathing, harsh and laborious. The clouds lifted. A little light came into the barn. The dog danced, barking, and the crouching man awoke, raising a haggard face.

'Thank God you've come,' he said. 'She can't breathe. She's got an awful pain in her chest, and a cough. She can't catch her breath, and she's burning. Help her, Doctor—Jolly Jumbo has left us high and dry.'

'What?' I said. 'Went on and left you here, all alone?'

'Quite right, Doctor.'

I said: 'I'm not a doctor.'

'Jumbo promised to send a doctor from the village,' the man said, with a laugh more unhappy than tears. 'Jolly Jumbo promised! I might have known. I did know. Jolly Jumbo never kept his word. Jumbo lives for hisself. But he didn't ought to leave us here in the rain, and Dolores in a bad fever. No, nobody's got the right. No!'

I said: 'You might have run down to Wettendene yourself, and got the doctor.'

' "Might" is a long word, mister. I've broke my ankle and my left wrist. Look at the mud on me, and see if I haven't tried... Third time, working my way on my elbows—and I am an agile man—I fainted with the pain, and half drowned in the mud...But Jumbo swore his Bible oath to send a physician for Dolores. Oh, dear me!'

At this the woman between short, agonised coughs, gasped: '*Alma de mi corazan*—heart of my soul—not leave? So cold, so hot, so cold. Please, not go?'

'I'll see myself damned first,' the man said, 'and so will Dot. Eh, Dot?'

At this the poodle barked and stood on its hindlegs, dancing.

The man said, drearily: 'She's a woman, do you see, sir. But one of the faithful kind. She come out of Mexico. That *alma de mi corazan*—she means it. Actually, it means 'soul of my heart'. There's nothing much more you can say to somebody you love, if you mean it... So you're not a doctor? More's the pity! I'd hoped you was. But oh, sir, for the sake of Christian charity, perhaps you'll give us a hand.

'She and me, we're not one of that rabble of layabouts, and gyppos, and what not. Believe me, sir, we're artists of our kind. I know that a gentleman like you doesn't regard us, because we live rough. But it would be an act of kindness for you to get a doctor up from Wettendene, because my wife is burning and coughing, and I'm helpless.

'I'll tell you something, guv'nor—poor little Dot, who understands more than the so-called Christians in these parts, she knew, *she* knew! She ran away. I called her: "Dot—Dot—Dot!"—but she run on. I'll swear she went for a doctor, or something.

'And in the meantime Jolly Jumbo has gone and left us high and dry. Low and wet is the better word, sir, and we haven't eaten this last two days.'

The girl, gripping his wrist, sighed: 'Please, not to go, not to leave?'

'Set your hear at ease, sweetheart,' the man said. 'Me and Dot, we are with you. And here's a gentleman who'll get us a physician. Because, to deal plainly with you, my one and only, I've got a bad leg now and a bad arm, and I can't make it through the mud to Wettendene. The dog tried and she come back with a bloody mouth where somebody kicked her...'

I said: 'Come on, my friends, don't lose heart. I'll run down to Wettendene and get an ambulance, or at least a doctor. Meanwhile,' I said, taking off my jacket, 'peel off some of those damp clothes. Put this on her. At least it's dry. Then I'll run down and get you some help.'

He said: 'All alone? It's a dretful thing, to be all alone. Dot'll go with you, if you will, God love you! But it's no use, I'm afraid.'

He said this in a whisper, but the girl heard him, and said, quite clearly: 'No use. Let him not go. Kind voice. Talk'—this between rattling gasps.

He said: 'All right, my sweet, he'll go in a minute.'

The girl said: 'Only a minute. Cold. Lonely—'

'What, Dolores, lonely with me and Dot?'

'Lonely, lonely, lonely.'

So the man forced himself to talk. God grant that no circumstances may compel any of you who read this to talk in such a voice. He was trying to speak evenly; but from time to time, when some word touched his heart, his voice broke like a boy's, and he tried to cover the break with a laugh that went inward, a sobbing laugh.

Holding the girl's hand and talking for her comfort, interrupted from time to time by the whimpering of the poodle Dot, he went on:

'They call me Alpha, you see, because my girl's name is Beta. That is her real name—short for Beatrice Dolores. But my real name is Alfred, and I come from Hampshire.

'They call us "tumblers", sir, but Dolores is an artist. I can do the forward rolls and the triple back-somersaults; but Dolores is the genius. Dolores, and that dog, Dot, do you see?

'It's a hard life, sir, and it's a rough life. I used to be a Joey—a kind of a clown—until I met Dolores in Southampton, where she'd been abandoned by a dago that run a puppet show, with side-shows, as went broke and left Dolores high and dry. All our lives, from Durham to Land's End, Carlisle to Brighton, north, south, east, west, I've been left high and dry when the rain came down and the money run out. Not an easy life, sir. A hard life, as a matter of fact. You earn your bit of bread, in this game.

'Ever since Dolores and me joined Jolly Jumnbo's Carnival, there was a run of bad luck. At Immersham, there was a cloudburst; Jumbo had took Grote's Meadow—we was two foot under water. The weather cleared at Athelboro' and they all came to see Pollux, the Strong Man, because, do you see, the blacksmith, at Athelboro' could lift an anvil over his head, and there was a fi'-pun prize for anybody who could out-lift Pollux (his name was really Michaels).

'Well, as luck would have it, at Athelboro' Pollux sprained his wrist. The blacksmith out-lifted him, and Jolly Jumbo told him to come back next morning for his fiver. We pulled out about midnight: Jumbo will never go to Athelboro' again. Then, in Pettydene, something happened to Gorgon, the man that eats bricks and swallows glass. His act was to bite lumps out of a brick, chew them up, wash them down with a glass of water, and crunch up and swallow the glass. We took the Drill Hall at Pettydene, and had a good house. And what happens, but Gorgon breaks a tooth!

'I tell you, sir, we had no luck. After that, at Firestone, something went wrong with the Mermaid. She was my property, you know—an animal they call a manatee—I bought her for a round sum from a man who caught her in South America. A kind of seal, but with breasts like a woman, and almost a human voice. She got a cough, and passed away.

'There was never such a round. Worst of all, just here, Dolores caught a cold.

'I dare say you've heard of my act, Alpha, Beta and Dot?... Oh, a stranger here; are you sir? I wish you could have seen it. Dolores is the genius—her and Dot. I'm only the under-stander. I would come rolling and somersaulting in, and stand. Then Dolores'd come dancing in and take what looked like a standing jump—I gave her a hand-up—on to my shoulders, so we stood balanced. Then, in comes poor little Dot, and jumps; first on to my shoulder, then on to Dolores' shoulder from mine, and so on to Dolores' head where Dot stands on her hind legs and dances...

'The rain comes down, sir. Dolores has got a cold in the chest. I beg her: "Don't go on, Dolores—don't do it!" But nothing will satisfy her, bless her heart: the show must go on. And when we come on, she was burning like a fire. Couldn't do the jump. I twist sidewise to take the weight, but her weight is kind of a deadweight, poor girl! My ankle snaps, and we tumbles.

'Tried to make it part of my act—making funny business, carrying the girl in my arms, hopping on one foot, with good old Dot dancing after us.

'That was the end of us in Wettendene. Jolly Jumbo says to us: "Never was such luck. The brick-eater's bust a tooth. The mermaid's good and dead. The strong-man has strained hisself ... and I'm not sure but that blacksmith won't be on my trail, with a few pals, for that fi'pun note. I've got to leave you to it, Alph, old feller, I'm off to Portsmouth."

'I said: "And what about my girl? I've only got one hand and one foot, and she's got a fever."

'He said: "Wait a bit, Alph, just wait a bit. My word of honour, and my Bible oath, I'll send a sawbones up from Wettendene."

' "And what about our pay?" I ask.

'Jolly Jumbo says: "I swear on my mother's grave, Alph, I haven't got it. But I'll have it in Portsmouth, on my Bible oath. You know me. Sacred word of honour! I'll be at The Hope and Anchor for a matter of weeks, and you'll be paid in full. And I'll send you a doctor, by my father's life I will. Honour bright! In the meantime, Alph, I'll look after Dot for you."

'And so he picked up the dog—I hadn't the strength to prevent him—and went out, and I heard the whips cracking and the vans squelching in the mud.

'But little Dot got away and came back...

'I've been talking too much, sir. I thought you was the doctor. Get one for the girl, if you've a heart in you—and a bit of meat for the dog. I've got a few shillings on me.'

I said: 'Keep still. I'll be right back.' And I ran in the rain, closely followed by the dog Dot, down through that dripping green tunnel into Wettendene, and rang long and loud at a black door to which was affixed the brass plate, well worn, of one Dr MacVitie, M.R.C.S., L.R.C.P.

The old doctor came out, brushing crumbs from his waistcoat. There was an air of decrepitude about him. He led me into his surgery. I saw a dusty old volume of Gray's Anatomy, two fishing rods, four volumes of the Badminton Library—all unused these past twenty years. There were also some glass-stoppered bottles that seemed to contain nothing but sediment; a spirit lamp without spirit; some cracked test-tubes; and an ancient case-book into the cover of which was stuck a rusty scalpel.

He was one of the cantankerous old Scotch school of doctors that seem incapable of graciousness, and grudging even of a civil word. He growled; 'I'm in luck this evening. It's six months since I sat down to my bit of dinner without the bell going before I had the first spoonful of soup half-way to my mouth. Well, you've let me finish my evening meal. Thank ye.'

He was ponderously ironic, this side of offensiveness. 'Well, out with it. What ails ye? Nothing, I'll wager. Nothing ever ails 'em hereabouts that a dose of castor oil or an aspirin tablet will not cure—excepting always rheumatism. Speak up, man!'

I said: 'There's nothing wrong with me at all. I've come to fetch you to treat two other people up at Wagnall's Barn. There's a man with a broken ankle and a girl with a congestion of the lungs. So get your bag and come along.'

He snapped at me like a turtle, and said: 'And since when, may I ask, were you a diagnostician? And who are you to be giving a name to symptoms? In any case, young fellow, I'm not practising. I'm retired. My son runs the practice, and he's out on a child-bed case... Damn that dog—he's barking again!'

The poodle, Dot, was indeed barking hysterically and scratching at the front door.

I said: 'Doctor, these poor people are in desperate straits.'

'Aye, poor people always are. And who's to pay the bill?'

'I'll pay,' I said, taking out my wallet.

'Put it up, man, put it up! Put your hand in your pocket for all the riff-raff that lie about in barns and ye'll end in the workhouse.'

He got up laboriously, sighing: 'Alex is over Iddlesworth way with the car. God give us strength to bear it. I swore my oath and so I'm bound to come, Lord preserve us!'

'If——' I said, 'if you happen to have a bit of meat in the house for the dog, I'd be glad to pay for it——'

'—And what do you take this surgery for? A butcher's shop? Then he paused. 'What sort of a dog, as a matter of curiosity, would ye say it was?'

'A little grey French poodle.'

'Oh, aye? Very odd. Ah well, there's a bit of meat on the chop bones, so I'll put 'em in my pocket for the dog, if you like... Wagnall's Barn, did ye say? A man and a girl, is that it? They'll be some kind of vagrant romanies, or gyppos, no doubt?'

I said: 'I believe they are some kind of travelling performers. They are desperately in need of help. Please hurry, Doctor.'

His face was sour and his voice harsh, but his eyes were bewildered, as he said: 'Aye, no doubt. I dare say, very likely. A congestion of the lungs, ye said? And a fractured ankle, is that it? Very well.' He was throwing drugs and bandages into his disreputable-looking black bag. I helped him into his immense black mackintosh.

He said: 'As for hurrying, young man, I'm seventy-seven years old, my arteries are hard, and I could not hurry myself for the crack of doom. Here, carry the bag. Hand me my hat and my stick, and we'll walk up to Wagnall's Barnon, this fool's errand of yours. Because a fool's errand it is, I fancy. Come on.'

The little dog, Dot, looking like a bit of the mud made animate, only half distinguishable in the half dark, barked with joy, running a little way backwards and a long way forwards, leading us back to the Barn through that darkened green tunnel.

The doctor had a flash-lamp. We made our way to the barn, he grumbling and panting and cursing the weather. We went in. He swung the beam of his lamp from corner to corner, until it came to rest on my jacket. It lay as I had wrapped it over poor Dolores, but it was empty.

I shouted: 'Alpha, Beta! Here's the doctor!'

The echo answered: *'Octor!'*

I could only pick up my jacket and say: 'They must have gone away.'

Dr MacVitie said, drily: 'Very likely, if they were here at all.'

'Here's my jacket, damp on the inside and dry on the outside,' I said. 'And I have the evidence of my own eyes——'

'No doubt. Very likely. In a lifetime of practice I have learned, sir, to discredit the evidence of my eyes, and my other four senses, besides. Let's away. Come!'

'But where have they gone?'

'Ah, I wonder!'

'And the dog, where's the dog?' I cried.

He said, in his dour way: 'For that, I recommend you consult Mr Lindsay, the vet.'

So we walked down again, without exchanging a word until we reached Dr MacVitie's door. Then he said: 'Where did you spend your evening?'

I said: 'I came straight to the Barn from The White Swan.'

'Well, then,' he said, 'I recommend ye go back, and take a whisky and water, warm; and get ye to bed in a dry nightshirt. And this time take a little more water with it. Goodnight to ye—,' and slammed the door in my face.

I walked the half mile to The White Swan, which was still open. The landlord, Mr Lagg, looked me up and down, taking notice of my soaking wet clothes and muddy boots. 'Been out?' he asked.

In Sussex they have a way of asking unnecessary, seemingly innocent questions of this nature which lead to an exchange of witticisms—for which, that night, I was not in the mood.

I said: 'I went up to Wagnall's Barn for Jolly Jumbo's Carnival but he pulled out, it seems, and left a man, a woman, and a dog—'

'You hear that, George?' said Mr Lagg to a very old farmer whose knobbed ash walking-stick seemed to have grown out of the knobbed root of his earthy, arthritic hand, and who was smoking a pipe mended in three places with insulating tape.

'I heerd,' said old George, with a chuckle. 'Dat gen'lemen'll been a liddle bit late for dat carnival, like.'

At this they both laughed. But then Mr Lagg said, soothingly, as to a cash customer: 'Didn't you look at the notice on the bill, sir? Jolly Jumbo was here all right, and flitted in a hurry too. And he did leave a man and a girl (not lawfully married, I heerd) and one o' them liddle shaved French dogs.

'I say, you'm a liddle late for Jolly Jumbo's Carnival, sir, 'cause if you look again at Jolly Jumbo's bill, you'll see—I think the programme for the Cricket Match covers up the corner—you'll see the date on it is August the fourteenth, 1904. I was a boy at the time; wasn't I, George?'

'Thirteen-year-old,' old George said, 'making you sixty–three to my seventy-two. Dat were a sad business, but as ye sow, so shall ye reap, they says. Live a vagabond, die a vagabond. Live in sin, die in sin—'

'All right, George,' said Mr Lagg, 'you're not in chapel now…I don't know how you got at it, sir, but Jolly Jumbo (as he called hisself) lef' two people and a dog behind. Hauled out his vans, eleven o'clock at night, and left word with Dr MacVitie (the old one, that was) to go up to Wagnall's Barn.

'But he was in the middle o' dinner, and wouldn't go. Then he was called out to the Squire's place, and didn't get home until twelve o'clock next night. And there was a liddle dog that kep' barking and barking, and trying to pull him up the path by the trousis-leg. But Dr MacVitie—'

'Dat were a mean man, dat one, sure enough!'

'You be quiet, George. Dr MacVitie kicked the liddle dog into the ditch, and unhooked the bell, and tied up the knocker, and went to bed. Couple o' days later, Wagnall, going over his land, has a look at that barn, and he sees a young girl stone dead, a young fellow dying, and a poor liddle dog crying fit to break your heart. Oh, he got old Dr MacVitie up to the barn then all right, but t'was too late. The fellow, he died in the Cottage Hospital.

'They tried to catch the dog, but nobody could. It stood off and on, like, until that pair was buried by the parish. Then it run off into the woods, and nobody saw it again——'

'Oh, but didn't they, though?' said old George.

Mr Lagg said: 'It's an old wives' tale, sir. They *do* say that this here liddle grey French dog comes back every year on August the fourteenth to scrat and bark at the doctor's door, and lead him to Wagnall's Barn. And be he in the middle of his supper or be he full, be he weary or rested, wet or dry, sick or well, go he must... *He* died in 1924, so you see it's nothing but an old wives' tale—'

'Dey did used to git light-headed, like, here on the marshes,' said old George, 'but dey do say old Dr MacVitie mustn't rest. He mus' pay dat call to dat empty barn, every year, because of his hard heart. Tomorrow, by daylight, look and see if doctor's door be'nt all scratted up, like.

'George, you're an old woman in your old age,' said Mr Lagg. 'We take no stock of such things in these parts, sir. Would you like to come up to the lounge and look at the television until closing time?'

The Mark of the Beast

RUDYARD KIPLING

East of Suez, some hold, the direct control of Providence ceases; Man being there handed over to the power of the Gods and Devils of Asia, and the Church of England Providence only exercising an occasional and modified supervision in the case of Englishmen.

This theory accounts for some of the more unnecessary horrors of life in India: it may be stretched to explain my story.

My friend Strickland of the police, who knows as much of natives of India as is good for any man, can bear witness to the facts of the case. Dumoise, our doctor, also saw what Strickland and I saw. The inference which he drew from the evidence was entirely incorrect. He is dead now; he died, in a rather curious manner, which has been elsewhere described.

When Fleete came to India, he owned a little money and some land in the Himalayas, near a place called Dharmsala. Both properties had been left him by an uncle, and he came out to finance them. He was a big, heavy, genial, and inoffensive man.

His knowledge of natives was, of course, limited, and he complained of the difficulties of the language.

He rode in from his place in the hills to spend New Year in the station, and he stayed with Strickland. On New Year's Eve there was a big dinner at the club, and the night was excusably wet. When men foregather from the uttermost ends of the Empire, they have a right to be riotous. The Frontier had sent down a contingent o' Catch-'em-Alive-O's who had not seen twenty white faces for a year, and were used to ride fifteen miles to dinner at the next Fort at the risk of a Khyberee bullet where their drinks should lie. They profited by their new security, for they tried to play pool with a curled-up hedgehog found in the garden, and one of them carried the marker round the room in his teeth. Half a dozen planters had come in from the south and were talking 'horse' to the Biggest Liar in Asia, who was trying to cap all their stories at once. Everybody was there, and there was a general closing up of ranks and taking stock of our losses in dead or disabled that had fallen during the past year.

It was a very wet night, and I remember that we sang 'Auld Lang Syne' with our feet in the Polo Championship Cup, and our heads among the stars, and swore that we were all dear friends. Then some of us went away and annexed Burma, and some tried to open up the Soudan and were opened up by Fuzzies in that cruel scrub outside Suakim, and some found stars and medals, and some were married, which was bad, and some did other things which were worse, and the others of us stayed in our chains and strove to make money on insufficient experiences.

Fleete began the night with sherry and bitters, drank champagne steadily up to dessert, then raw, rasping Capri with all the strength of whisky, took Benedictine with his coffee, four or five whiskies and sodas to improve his pool strokes, beer and bones at half-past two, winding up with old brandy. Consequently, when he came out, at half-past three in the morning, into fourteen degrees of frost, he was very angry with his horse for coughing, and tried to leapfrog into the saddle. The horse broke away and went to his stables; so Strickland and I formed a Guard of Dishonour to take Fleete home.

Our road lay through the bazaar, close to a little temple of Hanuman, the Monkey-god, who is a leading divinity worthy of respect. All gods have good points, just as have all priests. Personally, I attach much importance to Hanuman, and am kind to his people—the great gray apes of the hills. One never knows when one may want a friend.

There was a light in the temple, and as we passed, we could hear voices of men chanting hymns. In a native temple, the priests rise at all hours of the night to do honour to their god. Before we could stop him, Fleete dashed up the steps, patted two priests on the back, and was gravely grinding the ashes of his cigar butt into the forehead of the red stone image of Hanuman. Strickland tried to drag him out, but he sat down and said solemnly:

'Shee that? Mark of the B—beasht! *I* made it. Ishn't it fine?'

In half a minute the temple was alive and noisy, and Strickland, who knew what came of polluting gods, said that things might occur. He, by virtue of his official position, long residence in the country, and weakness for going among the natives, was known to the priests and he felt unhappy. Fleete sat on the ground and refused to move. He said that 'good old Hanuman' made a very soft pillow.

Then, without any warning, a Silver Man came out of a recess behind the image of the god. He was perfectly naked in that bitter, bitter cold, and his body shone like frosted silver, for he was what the Bible calls 'a leper as white as snow'. Also, he had no face, because he was a leper of some years' standing and his disease was heavy upon him. We two stooped to haul Fleete up, and the temple was filling and filling with folk who seemed to spring from the earth, when the Silver Man ran in under our arms, making a noise exactly like the mewing of an otter, caught Fleete round the body and dropped his head on Fleete's breast before we could wrench him away. Then he retired to a corner and sat mewing while the crowd blocked all the doors.

The priests were very angry until the Silver Man touched Fleete. That nuzzling seemed to sober them.

At the end of a few minutes' silence one of the priests came to Strickland and said, in perfect English, 'Take your friend away. He was done with Hanuman, but Hanuman has not done with him.' The crowd gave room and we carried Fleete into the road.

Strickland was very angry. He said that we might all three have been knifed, and that Fleete should thank his stars that he had escaped without injury.

Fleete thanked no one. He said that he wanted to go to bed. He was gorgeously drunk.

We moved on, Strickland silent and wrathful, until Fleete was taken with violent shivering fits and sweating. He said that the smells of the bazaar were overpowering, and he wondered why slaughter-houses were permitted so near English residences. 'Can't you smell the blood?' said Fleete.

We put him to bed at last, just as the dawn was breaking, and Strickland invited me to have another whisky and soda. While we were drinking, he talked of the trouble in the temple and admitted that it baffled him completely. Strickland hates being mystified by natives, because his business in life is to overmatch them with their own weapons. He has not yet succeeded in doing this, but in fifteen or twenty years he will have made some small progress.

'They should have mauled us,' he said, 'instead of mewing at us. I wonder what they meant. I don't like it one little bit.'

I said that the Managing Committee of the temple would in all probability bring a criminal action against us for insulting their religion. There was a section of the Indian Penal Code which exactly met Fleete's offense. Strickland said he only hoped and prayed that they would do this. Before I left I looked into Fleete's room and saw him lying on his right side, scratching his left breast. Then I went to bed—cold, depressed, and unhappy—at seven o'clock in the morning.

At one o'clock I rode over to Strickland's house to inquire after Fleete's head. I imagined that it would be a sore one. Fleete was breakfasting and seemed unwell. His temper was gone, for he was abusing the cook for not supplying him with an underdone chop. A man who can eat raw meat after a wet night is a curiosity. I told Fleete this and he laughed.

'You breed queer mosquitoes in these parts,' he said. 'I've been bitten to pieces, but only in one place.'

'Let's have a look at the bite,' said Strickland. 'It may have gone down since this morning.'

While the chops were being cooked, Fleete opened his shirt and showed us, just over his left breast, a mark, the perfect double of the black rosettes—the five or six irregular blotches arranged in a circle—on a leopard's hide. Strickland looked and said, 'It was only pink this morning. It's grown black now.'

Fleete ran to a glass.

'By Jove!' he said, 'this is nasty. What is it?'

We could not answer. Here the chops came in, all red and juicy, and Fleete bolted three in a most offensive manner. He ate on his right grinders only, and threw his head over his right shoulder as he snapped the meat. When he had finished, it struck him that he had been behaving strangely, for he said apologetically, 'I don't think I ever felt so hungry in my life. I've bolted like an ostrich.'

After breakfast Strickland said to me, 'Don't go. Stay here, and stay for the night.'

Seeing that my house was not three miles from Strickland's, this request was absurd. But Strickland insisted, and was going to say something when Fleete interrupted by declaring in a shamefaced way that he felt hungry again. Strickland sent a man to my house to fetch over my bedding and a horse, and we three went down to Strickland's stables to pass the hours until it was time to go out for a ride. The man who has a weakness for horses never wearies of inspecting them; and when two men are killing time in this way, they gather knowledge and lies the one from the other.

There were five horses in the stables, and I shall never forget the scene as we tried to look them over. They seemed to have gone mad. They reared and screamed and nearly tore up their pickets; they sweated and shivered and lathered and were distraught with fear. Strickland's horses used to know him as well as his dogs; which made the matter more curious. We left the stable for fear of the brutes throwing themselves in their panic. Then Strickland turned back and called me. The horses were still frightened, but they let us 'gentle' and make much of them, and put their heads in our bosoms.

'They aren't afraid of us,' said Strickland. 'D'you know, I'd give three months' pay if Outrage here could talk.'

But Outrage was dumb, and could only cuddle up to his master and blow out his nostrils, as is the custom of horses when they wish to explain things but can't. Fleete came up when we were in the stalls, and as soon as the horses saw him, their fright broke out afresh. It was all that we could do to escape from the place unkicked. Strickland said, 'They don't seem to love you, Fleete.'

'Nonsense,' said Fleete; 'my mare will follow me like a dog.' he went to her; she was in a loose-box; but as he slipped the bars she plunged, knocked him down, and broke away into the garden. I laughed, but Strickland was not amused. He took his moustache in both fists and pulled at it till it nearly came out. Fleete, instead of going off to chase his property, yawned, saying that he felt sleepy. He went to the house to lie down, which was a foolish way of spending New Year's Day.

Strickland sat with me in the stables and asked if I had noticed anything peculiar in Fleete's manner. I said that he ate his food like a beast; but that this might have been the result of living alone in the hills out of the reach of society as refined and elevating as ours for instance. Strickland was not amused. I do not think that he listened to me, for his next sentence referred to the mark on Fleete's breast, and I said that it might have been caused by blister-flies, or that it was possibly a birthmark newly born and now visible for the first time. We both agreed that it was unpleasant to look at, and Strickland found occasion to say that I was a fool.

'I can't tell you what I think now,' said he, 'because you would call me a madman; but you must stay with me for the next few days, if you can. I want you to watch Fleete, but don't tell me what you think till I have made up my mind.'

'But I am dining out tonight,' I said.

'So am I,' said Strickland, 'and so is Fleete. At least if he doesn't change his mind.'

We walked about the garden smoking, but saying nothing—because we were friends, and talking spoils good tobacco—till our pipes were out. Then we went to wake up Fleete. He was wide awake and fidgeting about his room.

'I say, I want some more chops,' he said. 'Can I get them?'

We laughed and said, 'Go and change. The ponies will be round in a minute.'

'All right,' said Fleete. 'I'll go when I get the chops—underdone ones, mind.'

He seemed to be quite in earnest. It was four o'clock, and we had had breakfast at one; still, for a long time, he demanded those underdone chops. Then he changed into riding clothes and went out into the verandah. His pony—the mare had not been caught—would not let him come near. All three horses were unmanageable—mad with fear—and finally Fleete said that he would stay at home and get something to eat. Strickland and I rode out wondering. As we passed the temple of Hanuman, the Silver Man came out and mewed at us.

'He is not one of the regular priests of the temple,' said Strickland. 'I think I should peculiarly like to lay my hands on him.'

There was no spring in our gallop on the racecourse that evening. The horses were stale, and moved as though they had been ridden out.

'The fright after breakfast has been too much for them,' said Strickland.

That was the only remark he made through the remainder of the ride. Once or twice I think he swore to himself; but that did not count.

We came back in the dark at seven o'clock and saw that there were no lights in the bungalow. 'Careless ruffians my servants are!' said Strickland.

My horse reared at something on the carriage drive, and Fleete stood up under its nose.

'What are you doing, grovelling about the garden?' said Strickland.

But both horses bolted and nearly threw us. We dismounted by the stables and returned to Fleete, who was on his hands and knees under the orange bushes.

'What the devil's wrong with you?' said Strickland.

'Nothing, nothing in the world,' said Fleete, speaking very quickly and thickly. 'I've been gardening—botanising you know. The smell of the earth is delightful. I think I'm going for a walk—a long walk—all night.'

Then I saw that there was something excessively out of order somewhere, and I said to Strickland, 'I am not dining out.'

'Bless you!' said Strickland. 'Here, Fleete, get up. You'll catch fever there. Come in to dinner and let's have the lamps lit. We'll all dine at home.'

Fleete stood up unwillingly, and said, 'No lamps—no lamps. It's much nicer here. Let's dine outside and have some more chops—lots of 'em and underdone—bloody ones with gristle.'

Now a December evening in Northern India is bitterly cold, and Fleete's suggestion was that of a maniac.

'Come in.' said Strickland sternly. 'Come in at once.'

Fleete came, and when the lamps were brought, we saw that he was literally plastered with dirt from head to foot. He must have been rolling in the garden. He shrank from the light and went to his room. His eyes were horrible to look at. There was a green light behind them, not in them, if you understand, and the man's lower lip hung down.

Strickland said, 'There is going to be trouble—big trouble—tonight. Don't change your riding things.'

We waited and waited for Fleete's reappearance, and ordered dinner in the meantime. We could hear him moving about his own room, but there was no light there. Presently, from the room came the long-drawn howl of a wolf.

People write and talk lightly of blood running cold and hair standing up and things of that kind. Both sensations are too horrible to be trifled with. My heart stopped as though a knife had been driven through it; and Strickland turned white as the tablecloth.

The howl was repeated, and was answered by another howl far across the fields.

That set the gilded roof on the horror. Strickland dashed into Fleete's room. I followed, and we saw Fleete getting out of the window. He made beast-noises in the back of his throat. He could not answer us when we shouted at him. He spat.

I don't quite remember what followed, but I think that Strickland must have stunned him with the long boot-jack or else I should never have been able to sit on his chest. Fleete could not speak, he could only snarl, and his snarls were those of a wolf, not of a man. The human spirit must have been giving way all day and have died out with the twilight. We were dealing with a beast that had once been Fleete.

The affair was beyond any human and rational experience. I tried to say 'hydrophobia', but the word wouldn't come, because I knew that I was lying.

We bound this beast with leather thongs of the punkah-rope, and tied its thumbs and big toes together, and gagged it with a shoehorn, which makes a very efficient gag if you know how to arrange it. Then we carried it into the dining room, and sent a man to Dumoise, the doctor, telling him to come over at once. After we had despatched the messenger and were drawing breath, Strickland said, 'It's no good. This isn't any doctor's work.' I, also, knew that he spoke the truth.

The beast's head was free, and it threw it about from side to side. Anyone entering the room would have believed that we were curing a wolf's pelt. That was the most loathsome accessory of all.

Strickland sat with his chin in the heel of his fist, watching the beast as it wriggled on the ground, but saying nothing. The shirt had been torn open in the scuffle and showed the black rosette mark on the left breast. It stood out like a blister.

In the silence of the watching we heard something without mewing like a she-otter. We both rose to our feet, and—I answer for myself, not Strickland—felt sick—actually and physically sick. We told each other, as did the men in *Pinafore,* that it was the cat.

Dumoise arrived, and I never saw a little man so unprofessionally shocked. He said that it was a heartrending case of hydrophobia and that nothing could be done. At least, any palliative measures would only prolong the agony. The beast was foaming at the mouth. Fleete, as we told Dumoise, had been bitten by dogs once or twice. Any man who keeps half a dozen terriers must expect a nip now and again. Dumoise could offer no help. He could only certify that Fleete was dying of hydrophobia. The beast was then howling, for it had managed to spit out the shoe-horn. Dumoise said that he would be ready to certify to the cause of death, and that the end was certain. He was a good little man, and he offered to remain with us; but Strickland refused the kindness. He did not wish to poison Dumoise's New Year. He would only ask him not to give the real cause of Fleete's death to the public.

So Dumoise left, deeply agitated; and as soon as the noise of the cartwheels had died away, Strickland told me, in a whisper, his suspicions. They were so wildly improbable that he dared not say them out aloud; and I, who entertained all Strickland's beliefs, was so ashamed of owning to them that I pretended to disbelieve.

'Even if the Silver Man had bewitched Fleete for polluting the image of Hanuman, the punishment could not have fallen so quickly.'

As I was whispering this the cry outside the house rose again, and the beast fell into a fresh paroxysm of struggling till we were afraid that the thongs that held it would give way.

'Watch!' said Strickland. 'If this happens six times I shall take the law into my own hands. I order you to help me.'

He went into his room and came out in a few minutes with the barrels of an old shotgun, a piece of fishing-line, some thick cord, and his heavy wooden bedstead. I reported that the convulsions had followed the cry by two seconds in each case, and the beast seemed perceptibly weaker.

Strickland muttered, 'But he can't take away the life! He can't take away the life!'

I said, though I knew that I was arguing against myself, 'It may be a cat. It must be a cat. If the Silver Man is responsible, why does he dare to come here?'

Strickland arranged the wood on the hearth, put the gun barrels into the glow of the fire, spread the twine on the table and broke a walking stick in two. There was one yard of fishing-line, gut, lapped with wire, such as is used for mahseer-fishing, and he tied the two ends together in a loop.

Then he said, 'How can we catch him? He must be taken alive and unhurt.'

I said that we must trust in Providence, and go out softly with polo sticks into the shrubbery at the front of the house. The man or animal that made the cry was evidently moving round the house as regularly as a night watchman. We could wait in the bushes till he came by and knock him over.

Strickland accepted this suggestion, and we slipped out from a bathroom window into the front verandah and then across the carriage drive into the bushes.

In the moonlight we could see the leper coming round the corner of the house. He was perfectly naked, and from time to time he mewed and stopped to dance with his shadow. It was an unattractive sight, and thinking of poor Fleete, brought to such degradation by so foul a creature, I put away all my doubts and resolved to help Strickland from the heated gun barrels to the loop of twine—from the loins to the head and back again—with all tortures that might be needful.

The leper halted in the front porch for a moment and we jumped out on him with the sticks. He was wonderfully strong, and we were afraid that he might escape or be fatally injured before we caught him. We had an idea that lepers were frail creatures, but this proved to be incorrect. Strickland knocked his legs from under him and I put my foot on his neck. He mewed hideously, and even through my riding boots I could feel that his flesh was not the flesh of a clean man.

He struck at us with his hand and feet-stumps. We looped the lash of a dog whip round him, under the armpits and dragged him backwards into the hall and so into the dining room where the beast lay. There we tied him with trunk straps. He made no attempt to escape, but mewed.

When we confronted him with the beast the scene was beyond description. The beast doubled backwards into a bow as though he had been poisoned with strychnine, and moaned in the most pitiable fashion. Several other things happened also, but they cannot be put down here.

'I think I was right,' said Strickland. 'Now, we will ask him to cure this case.'

But the leper only mewed. Strickland wrapped a towel round his hand and took the gun barrels out of the fire. I put the half of the broken walking stick through the loop of fishing-line and buckled the leper comfortably to Strickland's bedstead. I understood then how men and women and little children can endure to see a witch burnt alive; for, the beast was moaning on the floor, and though the Silver Man had no face, you could see horrible feeling passing through the slab that took its place, exactly as waves of heat play across red-hot iron—gun barrels for instance.

Strickland shaded his eyes with his hands for a moment and we got to work. This part is not to be printed.

The dawn was beginning to break when the leper spoke. His mewings had not been satisfactory up to that point. The beast had fainted from exhaustion and the house was very still. We unstrapped the leper and told him to take away the evil spirit. He crawled to the beast and laid his hand upon the left breast. That was all. Then he fell face down and whined, drawing in his breath as he did so.

We watched the face of the beast, and saw the soul of Fleete coming back into the eyes. Then a sweat broke out on the forehead, and the eyes—they were human eyes—closed. We waited for an hour but Fleete still slept. We carried him to his room and bade the leper go, giving him the bedstead and the sheet on the bedstead to cover his nakedness, the gloves and the towels with which we had touched him, and the whip that had been hooked round his body. He put the sheet about him and went out into the early morning without speaking or mewing.

Strickland wiped his face and sat down. A night-gong, far away in the city, made seven o'clock.

'Exactly four-and-twenty hours!' said Strickland. 'And, I've done enough to ensure my dismissal from the service, besides permanent quarters in a lunatic asylum. Do you believe that we are awake?'

The red-hot gun barrel had fallen on the floor and was singeing the carpet. The smell was entirely real.

That morning at eleven we two together went to wake up Fleete. We looked and saw that the black leopard-rosette on his chest had disappeared. He was very drowsy and tired, but as soon as he saw us, he said, 'Oh! Confound you fellows. Happy New Year to you. Never mix your liquors. I'm nearly dead.'

'Thanks for your kindness, but you're over time,' said Strickland. 'Today is the morning of the second. You've slept the clock round with a vengeance.'

The door opened and little Dumoise put his head in. He had come on foot, and fancied that we were laying out Fleete.

'I've brought a nurse,' said Dumoise. 'I suppose that she can come in for ... what is necessary.'

'By all means,' said Fleete cheerily, sitting up in bed. 'Bring on your nurses.'

Dumoise was dumb. Strickland led him out and explained that there must have been a mistake in the diagnosis. Dumoise remained dumb and left the house hastily. He considered that his professional reputation had been injured, and was inclined to make a personal matter of the recovery. Strickland went out, too. When he came back, he said that he had been to call on the Temple of Hanuman to offer redress for the pollution of the god, and had been solemnly assured that no white man had ever touched the idol and that he was an incarnation of all the virtues labouring under a delusion. 'What do you think?' said Strickland.

I said, '"There are more things ..."'

But Strickland hates that quotation. He says that I have worn it threadbare.

One other curious thing happened which frightened me as much as anything in all the night's work. When Fleete was dressed he came into the dining room and sniffed. He had a quaint trick of moving his nose when he sniffed. 'Horrid doggy smell, here,' said he. 'You should really keep those terriers of yours in better order. Try sulphur, Strick.'

But Strickland did not answer. He caught hold of the back of a chair, and, without warning, went into an amazing fit of hysterics. It is terrible to see a strong man overtaken with hysteria. Then, it struck me that we had fought for Fleete's soul with the Silver Man in that room, and had disgraced ourselves as Englishmen forever, and I laughed and gasped and gurgled just as shamefully as Strickland, while Fleete thought that we had both gone mad. We never told him what we had done.

Some years later, when Strickland had married and was a church-going member of society for his wife's sake, we reviewed the incident dispassionately, and Strickland suggested that I should put it before the public.

I cannot myself see that this step is likely to clear up the mystery; because, in the first place, no one will believe a rather unpleasant story, and, in the second, it is well-known to every right-minded man that the gods of the heathen are stone and brass, and any attempt to deal with them otherwise is justly condemned.

Henry

PHYLLIS BOTTOME

For four hours every morning and for twenty minutes before a large audience at night Fletcher was locked up with murder. It glared at him from twelve pairs of amber eyes; it clawed the air close to him, it spat naked hate at him, and watched with uninterrupted intensity to catch him for one moment off his guard.

Fletcher had only his will and his eyes to keep death at bay.

Of course, outside the cage into which Fletcher shut himself nightly with his twelve tigers were the keepers, standing at intervals around it with concealed pistols; but they were outside it. The idea was that if anything happened to Fletcher they would be able, by prompt action, to get him out alive; but they had his private instructions to do nothing of the kind, to shoot straight at his heart, and pick off the guilty tiger afterwards to cover their intention. Fletcher knew better than to try to preserve anything the tigers left of him, if once they had started in.

The lion-tamer in the next cage was better off than Fletcher, he was intoxicated by a rowdy vanity which dimmed fear. He stripped himself half naked every night, covered himself with ribbons, and thought so much of himself that he hardly noticed his lions. Besides, his lions had all been born in captivity, were slightly doped, and were only lions.

Fletcher's tigers weren't doped because dope dulled their fears of the whip and didn't dull their ferocity; captivity softened nothing in them, and they hated man.

Fletcher had taught tigers since he was a child; his father had started him on baby tigers, who were charming. They hurt you as much as they could with an absent-minded roguishness difficult to resist; what was death to you was play to them; but as they couldn't kill him, all the baby a loud, contented, pleasant noise. Henry was purring!

Fletcher's voice changed from the sharp brief order like the crack of a whip into a persuasive companionable drawl. Henry's eyes reopened; he rose, stood rigid for a moment, and then slowly the rigidity melted out of his powerful form. Once more that answering look came into the tiger's eyes. He stared straight at Fletcher without blinking and jumped on his tub. He sat on it impassively, his tail waving, his great jaws closed. He eyed Fletcher attentively and without hate. Then Fletcher knew that this tiger was not as other tigers, not as any other tiger.

He threw down his whip, Henry never moved; he approached; Henry lifted his lip to snarl, thought better of it, and permitted the approach. Fletcher took his life in his hand and touched Henry.

Henry snarled mildly, but his great claws remained closed; his eyes expressed nothing but a gentle warning; they simply said:

'You know I don't like being touched; be careful, I might have to claw you!' Fletcher gave a brief nod; he knew the margin of safety was slight, but he had a margin. He could do something with Henry.

Hour after hour, every day he taught Henry, but he taught him without a pistol or whip. It was unnecessary to use anything beyond his voice and his eyes. Henry read his eyes eagerly. When he failed to catch Fletcher's meaning, Fletcher's voice helped him out. Henry did not always understand even Fletcher's voice, but where he differed from the other tigers was that he wished to understand; nor had he from the first the slightest inclination to kill Fletcher.

He used to sit for hours at the back of his cage waiting for Fletcher. When he heard far off—unbelievably far off—the sound of Fletcher's step, he moved forward to the front of his cage and prowled restlessly to and fro till Fletcher unlocked the door and entered. Then Henry would crouch back a little, politely, from no desire to avoid his friend, but as a mere tribute to the superior power he felt in Fletcher. Directly Fletcher spoke, he came forward proudly and exchanged their wordless eye language.

Henry liked doing his tricks alone with Fletcher. He jumped on and off his tub following the mere wave of Fletcher's hand. He soon went further, jumped on a high stool and leapt through a large white paper disc held up by Fletcher. Although the disc looked as if he couldn't possibly get through it, yet the clean white sheet always yielded to his impact; he did get through it, blinking a little, but feeling a curious pride that he had faced the odious thing—and pleased Fletcher.

He let Fletcher sit on his back, though the mere touch of an alien creature was repulsive to him. But he stood perfectly still, his hair rising a little, his teeth bared, a growl half suffocated in his throat. He told himself it was Fletcher. He must control his impulse to fling him off and tear him up.

In all the rehearsals and performances in the huge arena, full of strange noises, blocked with alien human beings, Henry led the other tigers; and though Fletcher's influence over him was weakened, he still recognised it. Fletcher seemed farther away from him at these times, less sympathetic and godlike, but Henry tried hard to follow the intense persuasive eyes and the brief emphatic voice; he would not lose touch even with this attenuated ghost of Fletcher.

It was with Henry and Henry alone that Fletcher dared his nightly stunt, dropped the whip and stick at his feet and let Henry do his tricks as he did them in his cage alone, with nothing beyond Fletcher's eyes and voice to control him. The other eleven tigers, beaten, glaring and snarling on to their tubs, sat impassively despising Henry's unnatural docility. He had the chance they had always wanted, and he didn't take it—what kind of tiger was he?

But Henry ignored the other tigers. Reluctantly standing with all four feet together on his tub, he contemplated a further triumph. Fletcher stood before him, holding a stick between his hands and above his head, intimately, compellingly; through the language of his eyes Fletcher told Henry to jump from his tub over his head. What Fletcher said was: 'Come on, old tiling! Jump! Come on! I'll duck in time. You won't hurt me! It's my stunt! Stretch your old paws together and jump!'

And Henry jumped. He hated the dazzling lights, loathed the hard, unexpected, senseless sounds which followed his leap, and he was secretly terrified that he would land on Fletcher. But it was very satisfactory when, after his rush through the air, he found he hadn't touched Fletcher, but had landed on another tub carefully prepared for him; and Fletcher said to him as plainly as possible before he did the drawer trick with the other tigers: 'Well! You are a one-er, and no mistake!'

The drawer trick was the worst of Fletcher's stunts. He had to put a table in the middle of the cage and whip each tiger up to it. When he had them placed, each on his tub around the table, he had to feed them with a piece of raw meat deftly thrown at the exact angle to reach the special tiger for which it was intended, and to avoid contact with eleven other tigers ripe to dispute his intention. Fletcher couldn't afford the slightest mistake or a fraction of delay.

Each tiger had to have in turn his piece of raw meat, and the drawer shut after it—opened—the next morsel thrown exactly into the grasp of the next tiger, and so on until the twelve were fed.

Fletcher always placed Henry at his back. Henry snatched in turn his piece of raw meat, but he made no attempt, as the other tigers always did, to take anyone else's; and Fletcher felt the safer for knowing that Henry was at his back. He counted on Henry's power to protect him more than he counted on the four keepers standing outside the cage with their pistols. More than once, when one of the other tigers turned restive, Fletcher had found Henry rigid, but very light on his toes, close to his side, between him and danger.

The circus manager spoke to Fletcher warningly about his foolish infatuation for Henry.

'Mark my words, Fletcher,' he said, 'the tiger doesn't live that wouldn't do you in if it could. You give Henry too many chances—one day he'll take one of them.' But Fletcher only laughed. He knew Henry; he had seen the soul of the great tiger leap to his eyes and shine there in answer to his own eyes. A man does not kill his god; at least not willingly It is said that two thousand years ago he did some such thing, through ignorance, but Fletcher forgot this incident. Besides, on the whole, he believed more in Henry than he did in his fellow-men.

This was not surprising because Fletcher had very little time for human fellowship. When he was not teaching tigers not to kill him, he rested from the exhaustion of the nerves which comes from a prolonged companionship with eager, potential murders; and the rest of the time Fletcher boasted of Henry to the lion-tamer and taught Henry new tricks.

Macormack, the lion-tamer, had a very good stunt lion, and he was extravagantly jealous of Henry. He could not make his lion go out backwards before him from the arena cage into the passage as Henry had learned to do before Fletcher, and when he had tried, Ajax had, not seriously, but with an intention rather more than playful, flung him against the bars of the cage.

Macormack brooded deeply on this slight from his pet, and determined to take it out of Fletcher's.

'Pooh!' he said. 'You call yourself damned plucky for laying your ole 'oof on 'enry's scruff, and e' don't 'alf look wicked while you're doin' it. Why don't ye put yer 'ead in 'is mouf and be done with it? That 'ud be talking, that would!'

'I wouldn't mind doing it,' said Fletcher reflectively, after a brief pause, 'once I get him used to the idea. 'is jaw aint so big as a lion's, still I could get the top of me 'ead in.'

The lion-tamer swaggered off jeering, and Fletcher thought out how best to lay this new trick before Henry for his approval.

But from the first Henry didn't approve of it. He showed quite plainly that he didn't want his head touched. He didn't like his mouth held forcibly open, and wouldn't have anything put between his teeth without crunching. Fletcher wasted several loaves of bread over the effort—and only succeeded once or twice gingerly and very ungracefully in getting portions of his own head in and out in safety. Henry roared long and loudly at him, clawed the air, and flashed all the language he could from his flaming eyes into Fletcher's, to explain that this thing wasn't done between tigers! It was hitting below the belt! An infringement of an instinct too deep for him to master: and Fletcher knew that he was outraging Henry's instinct, and decided to refrain,

'It ain't fair to my tiger!' he said to himself regretfully; and he soothed Henry with raw meat and endearments, promising to refrain from his unnatural venture.

But when the hour for the performance came, Fletcher forgot his promise. He was enraged at Macormack's stunt lion for getting more than his share of the applause. He had the middle cage, and what with the way Macormack swaggered half naked in his scarlet ribbons, and the lion roared—the pulverising, deep-toned, desert roar—and yet did all his tricks one after the other like a little gentleman, it did seem as if Henry barely got a round of his due applause.

Henry jumped through his white disc—so did the stunt lion! He took his leap over Fletcher's head—the stunt lion did something flashy with a drum, not half as dangerous, and the blind and ignorant populace ignored Henry and preferred the drum.

'I don't care!' said Fletcher to himself, 'Henry's got to take my head in his mouth whether he likes it or not—that'll startle 'em!'

He got rid of all the other tigers. Henry was used to that, he liked it; now he would do his own final stunt—walk out backwards into the passage which led to the cages, and Fletcher would hurry out through the arena and back to Henry's cage, give him a light extra supper, and tell him what a fine tiger he was.

But Fletcher called him into *the* middle of the state instead, and made him take that terrible attitude he had taught him for the new trick. His eyes said: 'You'll do this once for me, old man, won't you?'

Henry's eyes said: 'Don't ask it! I'm tired! I'm hungry! I want to get out!'

But Fletcher wouldn't read Henry's eyes any more. He tried to force his head sideways into the terrible open jaws, and Henry's teeth, instinctive, reluctant, compelled, closed on Fletcher's neck.

What Henry minded after the momentary relief of his instinctive action was the awful stillness of Fletcher. It wasn't the stillness of the arena—that was nothing, a mere deep indrawn breath. Fletcher lay limp between his paws, as if the trick were over, as if all tricks were over. He wouldn't get up, he didn't look at Henry. Henry's eyes gazed down unblinkingly into the blank eyes of Fletcher. All Henry's soul was in his eyes, watching for Fletcher's soul to rise to meet them. And for an age nothing happened, until at last Henry realised that nothing ever would.

Before the nearest keeper shot Henry, Henry knew that he had killed his god. He lifted up his heavy painted head and roared out through the still arena, a loud despairing cry.

His heart was pierced before they reached his heart.

Mrs Amworth

E.F. Benson

The village of Maxley, where last summer and autumn these strange events took place, lies on a heathen and pine-clad upland of Sussex. In all England you could not find a sweeter and saner situation. Should the wind blow from the south, it comes laden with the spices of the sea; to the east, high downs protect it from the inclemencies of March; and from the west and north the breezes which reach it travel over miles of aromatic forest and heather. The village itself is insignificant enough in point of population, but rich in amenities and beauty. Half-way down the single street, with its broad road and spacious areas of grass on each side, stands the little Norman Church and the antique graveyard long disused: for the rest there are a dozen small, sedate Georgian houses, red-bricked and long-windowed, each with a square of flower garden in front, and an ampler strip behind; a score of shops, and a couple of score of thatched cottages belonging to labourers on neighbouring estates, complete the entire cluster of its peaceful habitations. The general peace, however, is sadly broken on Saturdays and Sundays, for we lie on one of the main roads between London and Brighton and our quiet street becomes a race-course for Hying motor-cars and bicycles. A notice just outside the village begging them to go slowly only seems to encourage them to accelerate, for the road lies open and straight, and there is really no reason why they should do otherwise. By way of protest, therefore, the ladies of Maxley cover their noses and mouths with their handkerchiefs as they see a motor-car approaching, though, as the street is asphalted, they need not really take these precautions against dust. But late on Sunday night the horde of scorchers has passed, and we settle down again to five days of cheerful and leisurely seclusion. Railway strikes which agitate the country so much leave us undisturbed because most of the inhabitants of Maxley never leave it at all.

I am the fortunate possessor of one of these small Georgian houses, and consider myself no less fortunate in having so interesting and stimulating a neighbour as Francis Urcombe, who, the most confirmed of Maxleyites, has not slept away from his house, which stands just opposite to mine in the village street, for nearly two years, at which date, though still in middle life he resigned his Physiological Professorship at Cambridge University, and devoted himself to the study of those occult and curious phenomena which seem equally to concern the physical and psychical sides of human nature. Indeed his retirement was not unconnected with his passion for the strange uncharted places that lie on the confines and borders of science, the existence of which is so stoutly denied by the more materialistic minds, for he advocated that all medical students should be obliged to pass some sort of examination in mesmerism, and that one of the tripos papers should be designed to test their knowledge in such subjects as appearances at the time of death, haunted houses, vampirism, automatic writing, and possession.

'Of course they wouldn't listen to me,' ran his account of the matter, 'for there is nothing that these seats of learning are so frightened of as knowledge, and the road to knowledge lies in the study of things like these. The functions of the human frame are, broadly speaking, known. They are a country, anyhow, that has been charted and mapped out. But outside that lie huge tracts of undiscovered terrain, which certainly exist, and the real pioneers of knowledge are those who, at the cost of being derided as credulous and superstitious, want to push on into those misty and probably perilous places. I felt that I could be of more use by setting out without compass or knapsack into the mists than by sitting in a cage like a canary and chirping about what was known. Besides, teaching is very bad for a man who knows himself only to be a learner: you only need to be a self-conceited ass to teach.'

Here, then, in Francis Urcombe, was a delightful neighbour to one who, like myself, has an uneasy and burning curiosity about what he called the 'misty and perilous places', and this last spring we had a further and most welcome addition to our pleasant little community, in the person of Mrs Amworth, widow of an Indian civil servant. Her husband had been a judge in the North-West Provinces, and after his death at Peshawar she came back to England, and after a year in London found herself starving for the ampler air and sunshine of the country to take the place of the fog and griminess of town. She had, too, a special reason for settling in Maxley, since her ancestors up until a hundred years ago had long been native to the place, and in the old churchyard, now disused, are many gravestones bearing her maiden name of Chaston. Big and energetic, her vigorous and genial personality speedily woke Maxley up to a higher degree of sociality than it ever had known. Most of us were bachelors or spinsters or elderly folk not much inclined to exert ourselves in the expense and effort of hospitality, and hitherto the gaiety of a small tea party, with bridge afterwards and galoshes (when it was wet) to trip home in again for a solitary dinner, was about the climax of our festivities. But Mrs Amworth showed us a more gregarious way, and set an example of luncheon parties and little dinners, which we began to follow. On other nights when no such hospitality was on foot, a lone man like myself found it pleasant to know that a call on the telephone to Mrs Amworth's house, not a hundred yards off, and an inquiry as to whether I might come over after dinner for a game of piquet before bedtime would probably evoke a response of welcome. There she would be, with comrade-like eagerness for companionship, and there was a glass of port and a cup of coffee and a cigarette and a game of piquet. She played the piano too, in a free and exuberant manner, and had a charming voice and sang to her own accompaniment; and as the days grew long and the light lingered late, we played our game in her garden, which in the course of a few months she had turned from being a nursery for slugs and snails into a glowing patch of luxuriant blossomings. She was always cheery and jolly; she was interested in everything; and in music, in gardening, in games of all sorts was a competent performer. Everybody (with one exception) liked her, everybody found her bringing with her the tonic of a sunny day. That one exception was Francis Urcombe; he, though he confessed he did not like her, acknowledged that he was vastly interested in her.

This always seemed strange to me, for pleasant and jovial as she was, I could see nothing in her that could call forth conjecture or intrigued surmise, so healthy and unmysterious a figure did she present. But of the genuineness of Urcombe's interest there could be no doubt; one could see him watching and scrutinising her. In the matter of age, she frankly volunteered the information that she was forty-five; but her briskness, her activity, her unravaged skin, her coal-black hair, made it difficult to believe that she was not adopting an unusual device and adding ten years on to her age instead of subtracting them.

Often, also, as our quite unsentimental friendship ripened, Mrs Amworth would ring me up and propose her advent. If I was busy writing, I was to give her, so we definitely bargained, a frank negative, and in answer I could hear her jolly laugh and her wishes for a successful evening of work. Sometimes, before her proposal arrived, Urcombe would already have stepped across from his house opposite for a smoke and a chat, and he, hearing who my intended visitor was, always urged me to beg her to come. She and I should play our piquet, said he, and he would look on, if we did not object and learn something of the game. But I doubt whether he paid much attention to it, for nothing could be clearer than that, under that penthouse of forehead and thick eyebrows, his attention was fixed not on the cards, but on one of the players. But he seemed to enjoy an hour spent thus, and often, until one particular evening in July, he would watch her with the air of a man who has some deep problem in front of him. She, enthusiastically keen about our game, seemed not to notice his scrutiny. Then came that evening when, as I see in the light of subsequent events, began the first twitching of the veil that hid the secret horror from my eyes. I did not know it then, though I noticed that thereafter if she rang up to propose coming round, she always asked not only if I was at leisure; but whether Mr Urcombe was with me. If so, she said, she would not spoil the chat of two old bachelors, and laughingly wished me goodnight. Urcombe, on this occasion, had been with me for some half-hour before Mrs Amworth's appearance, and had been talking to me about the medieval beliefs concerning vampirism, one of those border-land subjects which he declared had not been sufficiently studied before it had been consigned by the medical profession to the dustheap of exploded superstitions. There he sat, grim and eager, tracing with that pellucid clearness which had made him in his Cambridge days so admirable a lecturer, the history of those mysterious visitations. In them all there was the same general features; one of those ghoulish spirits took up its abode in a living man or woman, conferring supernatural powers of bat-like flight and glutting itself with nocturnal blood-feasts. When its host died, it continued to dwell in the corpse, which remained undecayed. By day it rested, by night it left the grave and went on its awful errands. No European country in the Middle Ages seemed to have escaped them; earlier yet, parallels were to be found in Roman and Greek and in Jewish history.

'It's a large order to set all that evidence aside as being moonshine,' he said. 'Hundreds of totally independent witnesses in many ages have testified to the occurrence of these phenomena, and there's no explanation known to me which covers all the facts. And if you feel inclined to say "Why, then, if these are facts, do we not come across them now?" there are two answers I can make you. One is that there were diseases known in the Middle Ages, such as the black death, which were certainly existent then and which have become extinct since, but for that reason we do not assert that such diseases never existed. Just as the black death visited England and decimated the population of Norfolk, so here in this very district, about three hundred years ago, there was certainly an outbreak of vampirism, and Maxley was the centre of it. My second answer is even more convincing, for I tell you that vampirism is by no means extinct now. An outbreak of it certainly occurred in India a year or two ago.'

At that moment I heard my knocker plied in the cheerful and peremptory manner in which Mrs Amworth is accustomed to announce her arrival, and I went to the door to open it.

'Come in at once,' I said, 'and save me from having my blood curdled. Mr Urcombe has been trying to alarm me.'

Instantly her vital, voluminous presence seemed to fill the room.

'Ah, but how lovely!' she said. 'I delight in having my blood curdled. Go on with your ghost story, Mr Urcombe. I adore ghost stories.'

I saw that, as his habit was, he was intently observing her.

'It wasn't a ghost story exactly,' said he. 'I was only telling our host how vampirism was not extinct yet. I was saying that there was an outbreak of it in India only a few years ago.'

There was a more than perceptible pause, and I saw that, if Urcombe was observing her, she on her side was observing him with fixed eye and parted mouth. Then her jolly laugh invaded that rather tense silence.

'Oh, what a shame!' she said. 'You're not going to curdle my blood at all. Where did you pick up such a tale, Mr Urcombe? I have lived for years in India and never heard a rumour of such a thing. Some storyteller in the bazaars must have invented it; they are famous at that.'

I could see that Urcombe was on the point of saying something further, but checked himself.

'Ah! Very likely that was it,' he said.

But something had disturbed our usual peaceful sociability that night, and something had dampened Mrs Amworth's usual high spirits. She had no gusto for her piquet, and left after a couple of games. Urcombe had been silent too, indeed he hardly spoke again until she departed.

'That was unfortunate,' he said, 'for the outbreak of a very mysterious disease, let us call it, took place at Peshawar where she and her husband were. And—'

'Well?' I asked.

'He was one of the victims of it' said he. 'Naturally I had quite forgotten that when I spoke.'

The summer was unreasonably hot and rainless, and Maxley suffered much from drought, and also from a plague of big black night-flying gnats, the bite of which was very irritating and virulent. They came sailing in on an evening, settling on one's skin so quietly that one perceived nothing until the sharp stab announced that one had been bitten. They did not bite the hands or face, but chose always the neck and throat for their feeding-ground, and most of us, as the poison spread, assumed a temporary goitre. Then about the middle of August appeared the first of those mysterious cases of illness which our local doctor attributed to the long-continued heat coupled with the bite of these venomous insects. The patient was a boy of sixteen or seventeen, the son of Mrs Amworth's gardener, and the symptoms were an anaemic pallor and a languid prostration, accompanied by great drowsiness and an abnormal appetite. He had, too, on his throat two small punctures where, so Dr Ross conjectured, one of these great gnats had bitten him. But the odd thing was that there was no swelling or inflammation round the place where he had been bitten. The heat at this time had begun to abate, but the cooler weather failed to restore him, and the boy, in spite of the quantity of food which he so ravenously swallowed, wasted away to a skinclad skeleton.

I met Dr Ross in the street one afternoon about this time, and in answer to my inquiries about his patient he said that he was afraid the boy was dying. The case, he confessed, completely puzzled him: some obscure form of pernicious anaemia was all he could suggest. But he wondered whether Mr Urcombe would consent to see the boy, on the chance of his being able to throw some new light on the case, and since Urcombe was dining with me that night, I proposed to Dr Ross to join us. He could not do this, but said he would look in later. When he came, Urcombe at once consented to put his skill at the other's disposal, and together they went off at once. Being thus shorn of my sociable evening, I telephoned Mrs Amworth to know if I might inflict myself on her for an hour. Her answer was a welcoming affirmative, and between piquet and music the hour lengthened itself into two. She spoke of the boy who was so desperately and mysteriously ill, and told me that she had often been to see him, taking him nourishing and delicate food. But today—and her kind eyes moistened as she spoke—she was afraid she had paid her last visit. Knowing the antipathy between her and Urcombe, I did not tell her that he had been called into consultation; and when I returned home she accompanied me to the door, for the sake of a breath of night air, and in order to borrow a magazine which contained an article on gardening which she wished to read.

'Ah, this delicious night air,' she said, luxuriously sniffing in the coolness. 'Night air and gardening are the great tonics. There is nothing so stimulating as bare contact with rich mother earth. You are never so fresh as when you have been grubbing in the soil—black hands, black nails, and boots covered with mud.' She gave her great jovial laugh.

'I'm a glutton for air and earth,' she said. 'Positively I look forward to death, for then I shall be buried and have the kind earth all round me. No leaden caskets for me—I have given explicit directions. But what shall I do about air? Well, I suppose one can't have everything. The magazine? A thousand thanks, I will faithfully return it. Good-night: garden and keep your windows open, and you won't have anaemia.'

'I always sleep with my windows open,' said I.

I went straight up to my bedroom, of which one of the windows looks out over the street, and as I undressed I thought I heard voices talking outside not far away. But I paid no particular attention, put out my lights, and falling asleep plunged into the depths of a most horrible dream, distortedly suggested, no doubt, by my last words with Mrs Amworth. I dreamed that I awoke, and found that both my bedroom windows were shut. Half-suffocating, I dreamed that I sprang out of bed, and went across to open them. The blind over the first one was drawn down, and pulling it up I saw, with the indescribable horror of incipient nightmare, Mrs Amworth's face suspended close to the pane in the darkness outside, nodding and smiling at me. Pulling down the blind again to keep that terror out, I rushed to the second window on the other side of the room, and there again was Mrs Amworth's face. Then the panic came upon me in full blast; here was I suffocating in the airless room, and whichever window I opened Mrs Amworth's face would float in. The nightmare rose to screaming point, and with strangled yells I awoke to find my room cool and quiet with both windows open and blinds up and a half-moon high in its course, casting an oblong of tranquil light on the floor. But even when I was awake, the horror persisted, and I lay tossing and turning. I must have slept long before the nightmare seized me, for now it was nearly day, and soon in the east the drowsy eyelids of morning began to lift.

I was scarcely downstairs next morning—for after the dawn I slept late—when Urcombe rang up to know if he might see me immediately. He came in, grim and preoccupied, and I noticed that he was pulling on a pipe that was not even filled.

'I want your help,' he said, 'and so I must tell you first of all what happened last night. I went round with the little doctor to see his patient, and found him just alive, but scarcely more. I instantly diagnosed in my own mind what this anaemia, unaccountable by any other explanation, meant. The boy is the prey of a vampire.'

He put his empty pipe on the breakfast table, by which I had just sat down, and folded his arms, looking at me steadily from under his overhanging brows.

'Now about last night,' he said. 'I insisted that he should be moved from his father's cottage into my house. As we were carrying him on a stretcher, whom should we meet but Mrs Amworth! She expressed shocked surprise that we were moving him. Now why do you think she did that?'

With a start of horror, as I remembered my dream that night before, I felt an idea come into my mind so preposterous and unthinkable that I instantly turned it out again.

'I haven't the smallest idea,' I said.

'Then listen, while I tell you about what happened later. I put out all the lights in the room where the boy lay, and watched. One window was a little open, for I had forgotten to close it, and about midnight I heard something outside, trying apparently to push it farther open. I guessed who it was—yes, it was full twenty feet from the ground—and I peeped round the corner of the blind. Just outside was the face of Mrs Amworth and her hand was on the frame of the window. Very softly I crept close, and then banged the window down, and I think I just caught the tip of one of her fingers.'

'But it's impossible,' I cried. 'How could she be floating in the air like that? And what had she come for? Don't tell me such—'

Once more, with closer grip, the remembrance of my nightmare seized me.

'I am telling you what I saw,' said he. 'And all night long, until it was nearly day, she was fluttering outside like some terrible bat, trying to gain admittance. Now put together various things I have told you.'

He began checking them off on his fingers.

'Number one,' he said: 'there was an outbreak of disease similar to that which this boy is suffering from at Peshawar, and her husband died of it. Number two: Mrs Amworth protested against my moving the boy to my house. Number three: she or the demon that inhabits her body, a creature powerful and deadly, tries to gain admittance. And add this, too: in medieval times there was an epidemic of vampirism here at Maxley. The vampire, so the accounts run, was found to be Elizabeth Chaston.... I see you remember Mrs Amworth's maiden name. Finally, the boy is stronger this morning. He would certainly not have been alive if he had been visited again. And what do you make of it?'

There was a long silence, during which I found this incredible horror assuming the hues of reality.

'I have something to add,' I said, 'which may or may not bear on it. You say that the—spectre went away shortly before dawn?'

'Yes.'

I told him of my dream, and he smiled grimly.

'Yes, you did well to awake,' he said. 'That warning came from your subconscious self, which never wholly slumbers, and cried out to you of deadly danger. For two reasons, then you must help me: one to save others, the second to save yourself

'What do you want me to do?' I asked.

'I want you first of all to help me in watching this boy, and ensuring that she does not come near him. Eventually I want you to help me in tracking the thing down, in exposing and destroying it. It is not human: it is an incarnate fiend. What steps we shall have to take I don't know.'

It was now eleven of the forenoon, and presently I went across to his house for a twelve-hour vigil while he slept, to come on duty again that night, so that for the next twenty-four hours either Urcombe or myself was always in the room where the boy, now getting stronger every hour, was lying. The day following was Saturday and a morning of brilliant pellucid weather, and already when I went across to his house to resume my duty, the stream of motors down to Brighton had begun. Simultaneously I saw Urcombe with a cheerful face, which boded good news of his patient, coming out of his house, and Mrs Amworth, with a gesture of salutation to me, and a basket in her hand, walking up the broad strip of grass which bordered the road. There we all three met. I noticed (and saw that Urcombe noticed it too) that one finger on her left hand was bandaged.

'Good morning to you both,' said she. 'And I hear your patient is doing well, Mr Urcombe. I have come to bring him a bowl of jelly, and to sit with him for an hour. He and I are great friends. I am overjoyed at his recovery.'

Urcombe paused a moment, as if making up his mind, and then shot out a pointing finger at her.

'I forbid that,' he said. 'You shall not sit with him or see him. And you know the reason as well as I do.'

I have never seen so horrible a change pass over a human face as that which now blanched hers to the colour of grey mist. She put up her hand as if to shield herself from the pointing finger, which drew the sign of the cross in the air, and shrank back cowering on the road. There was a wild hoot from a horn, a grinding of brakes, a shout—too late—from a passing car, and one long scream suddenly cut short. Her body rebounded from the roadway after the first wheel had gone over it, and the second followed it. It lay there, quivering and twitching and was still.

She was buried three days afterwards in the cemetery outside Maxley, in accordance with the wishes she had told me that she had devised about her internment, and the shock which her sudden and awful death had caused to the little community began by degrees to pass off. To two people only, Urcombe and myself, the horror of it was mitigated from the first by the nature of the relief that her death brought; but, naturally enough, we kept our own counsel, and no hint of what greater horror had been thus averted was ever let slip. But, oddly enough, so it seemed to me, he was still not satisfied about something in çonnnection with her, and would give no answer to my questions on the subject.

Then as the days of a tranquil mellow September and the October that followed began to drop away like the leaves of the yellowing trees, his uneasiness relaxed. But before the entry of November the seeming tranquillity broke into a hurricane.

I had been dining one night at the far end of the village, and about eleven o'clock was walking home again. The moon was of an unusual brilliance, rendering all that it shone on as distinct as in some etching. I had just come opposite the house which Mrs Amworth had occupied, where there was a board up saying that it was to let, when I heard the click of her front gate, and the next moment I saw, with a sudden chill and quaking of my very spirit, that she stood there. Her profile vividly illuminated, was turned to me, and I could not be mistaken in my identification of her. She appeared not to see me (indeed the shadow of the yew hedge in front of her garden enveloped me in its blackness), and she went swiftly across the road and entered the gate of the house directly opposite. There I lost sight of her completely.

My breath was coming in short pants as if I had been running—and now indeed I ran, with fearful backward glances, along the hundred yards that separated me from my house and Urcombe's. It was to his that my flying steps took me, and next minute I was within.

'What have you come to tell me?' he asked. 'Or shall I guess?'

'You can't guess.' said I.

'No; it's no guess. She has come back and you have seen her. Tell me about it.

I gave my story.

'That's Major Pearsall's house,' he said. 'Come back with me there at once.'

'But what can we do?' I asked.

'I've no idea. That's what we have got to find out,'

A minute later, we were opposite the house. When I had passed it before, it was all dark; now lights gleamed from a couple of windows upstairs. Even as we faced it, the front door opened, and next moment Major Pearsall emerged from the gate. He saw us and stopped.

'I'm on my way to Dr Ross,' he said quickly. 'My wife has been taken suddenly ill. She had been in bed an hour when I came upstairs, and found her white as a ghost and utterly exhausted. She had been to sleep, it seemed—But you will excuse me.'

'One moment, Major,' said Urcombe. 'Was there any mark on her throat ?'

'How did you guess that?' said he. 'There was; one of those beastly gnats must have bitten her twice there. She was streaming with blood.'

'And there's someone with her?' asked Urcombe.

'Yes, I roused her maid.'

He went off, and Urcombe turned to me. 'I know now what we have to do,' he said. 'Change your clothes, and I'll join you at your house.'

'What is it?' I asked.

'I'll tell you on our way. We're going to the cemetery.'

He carried a pick, a shovel, and a screwdriver when he rejoined me, and wore round his shoulders a long coil of rope. As we walked, he gave me the outlines of the ghastly hour that lay before us.

'What I have to tell you,' he said, 'will seem to you now too fantastic for credence, but before dawn we shall see whether it outstrips reality. By a most fortunate happening, you saw the spectre, the astral body, whatever you choose to call it, of Mrs

Amworth going on its grisly business, and therefore, beyond doubt, the vampire spirit which abode in her during life animates her again in death. That is not exceptional—indeed, all these weeks since her death I have been expecting it. If I am right, we shall find her body undecayed and untouched by corruption.'

'But she has been dead nearly two months,' said I.

'If she had been dead two years it would still be so, if the vampire has possession of her. So remember: whatever you see done, it will be done not to her, who in the natural course would now be feeding the grasses above her grave, but to a spirit of untold evil and malignancy, which gives a phantom life to her body.'

'But what shall I see done?' said I.

'I will tell you. We know that now, at this moment, the vampire clad in her mortal semblance is out; dining out. But it must get back before dawn, and it will pass into the material form that lies in her grave. We must wait for that, and then with your help I shall dig up her body. If I am right, you will look on her as she was in life, with the full vigour of the dreadful nutriment she has received pulsing in her veins. And then, when dawn has come, and the vampire cannot leave the lair of her body, I shall strike her with this'—and he pointed to his pick—'through the heart, and she, who comes to life again only with the animation the fiend gives her, she and her hellish partner will be dead indeed. Then we must bury her again, delivered at last.'

We had come to the cemetery, and in the brightness of the moonshine there was no difficulty in identifying her grave. It lay some twenty yards from the small chapel, in the porch of which, obscured by shadow, we concealed ourselves. From there we had a clear and open sight of the grave, and now we must wait until its infernal visitor returned home. The night was warm and windless, yet even if a freezing wind had been raging I think I should have felt nothing of it, so intense was my preoccupation as to what the night and dawn would bring. There was a bell in the turret of the chapel that struck the quarters of the hour, and it amazed me to find how swiftly the chimes succeeded one another.

The moon had long set but a twilight of stars shone in a clear sky, when five o'clock of the morning sounded from the turret. A few minutes more passed, and then I felt Urcombe's hand softly nudging me; and looking out in the direction of his pointing finger, I saw that the form of a woman, tall, and large in build, was approaching from the right. Noiselessly, with a motion more of gliding and floating than walking, she moved across the cemetery to the grave which was the centre of our observation. She moved round as if to be certain of its identity, and for a moment stood directly facing us. In the greyness, to which my eyes had now grown accustomed, I could easily see her face, and recognise its features.

She drew her hand across her mouth as if wiping it, and broke into a chuckle of such laughter as made my hair stir on my head. Then she leaped onto the grave, holding her hands high above her head, and inch by inch disappeared into the earth. Urcombe's hand was laid on my arm, in an injunction to keep still, but now he removed it.

'Come,' he said.

With pick and shovel and rope we went to the grave. The earth was light and sandy, and soon after six struck, we had delved down to the coffin lid. With his pick he loosened the earth around it, and, adjusting the rope through the handles by which it had been lowered, we tried to raise it. This was a long and laborious business, and the light had begun to herald day in the east before we had it out and lying by the side of the grave. With his screwdriver he loosened the fastenings of the lid, and slid it aside, and standing there we looked on the face of Mrs Amworth. The eyes, once closed in death, were open, the cheeks were flushed with colour, the red, full-lipped mouth seemed to smile.

'One blow and it is all over,' he said. 'You need not look.'

Even as he spoke he took up the pick again, and laying the point of it on her left breast, measured his distance. And though I knew what was coming I could not look away…

He grasped the pick in both hands, raised it an inch or two for the taking of his aim, and then with full force brought it down on her breast, A fountain of blood, though she had been dead so long, spouted high in the air, falling with the thud of a heavy splash over the shroud, and simultaneously from those red lips came one long, appalling cry, swelling up like some hooting siren, and dying away again, With that, instantaneous as a lightning flash, came the touch of corruption on her face, the colour of it faded to ash, the plump cheeks fell in, the mouth dropped.

'Thank God, that's over,' said he, and without pause slipped the coffin lid back into its place.

Day was coming fast now, and, working like men possessed, we lowered the coffin into its place again, and shovelled the earth over it... The birds were busy with their earliest pipings as we went back to Maxley.